small stations fiction

Xavier Queipo

Kite

Published in 2018 by
SMALL STATIONS PRESS
20 Dimitar Manov Street, 1408 Sofia, Bulgaria
You can order books and contact the publisher at
www.smallstations.com

This book was first published in the Galician language as *Papaventos*
by Edicións Xerais de Galicia (Vigo, 2001). A list of our fiction titles
can be found at www.smallstations.com/fiction

ISBN 978-954-384-088-5

Xavier Queipo

Kite

Translated from Galician by **Kirsty Hooper**

S m a l l
Stations
Press

For Adolfo and Fernando, who read the first draft,
who were critical and open,
who gave me the strength to carry on writing.

For the Kinneen family, who welcomed me into their house in
Galway, where I dreamed this story.

Gustavo Guerrero says that "the kingfisher dies blind".
They dive so often into the water that they burn their eyelids.
He was told this by a fisherman from La Laguna de la
Restinga, on the Island of Margarita.

Severo Sarduy, *Cocuyo*

I

They had met in the cinema. In one of those enormous auditoriums you hardly ever see any more. It was a screening of *Apocalypse Now*, Coppola's poignant parable based on Conrad's *Heart of Darkness*. During the scene when the helicopters advance on the Vietcong to the rhythm of Wagner, the auditorium filled with light from the napalm explosions. That was the first time they saw one another, when the shadows gave way to light. That was when she said, instinctive and sincere, with the cool assurance of women who know themselves to be builders of dreams:

"Let me hold your hand. I feel kind of shaky."

"Sure. Don't worry. I will be here till the end of the film," Francis replied with unexpected confidence.

They sat there holding hands, focused on the screen and glancing at each other only occasionally: looking at each other and feeling good. One beside the other. The other beside the one. Together. Hands entwined. Lives shot through by an invisible arrow. Presumably happy.

When they left the cinema, hands permanently entwined, kissing every now and again, stopping every few steps to gaze at one another, to make sure the earth wasn't moving beneath their feet, to reassure themselves that reality was still there, just as they had dreamed and contemplated it, astonishing and close to perfection, a more intimate knowledge seemed to exist between them, more history and more harmony than between any of the couples who have ever lived. Some people have a name, a label for this kind of instant passion (or perhaps all passion is instant in some way, stopping time and marking out a before and an after). Rose spoke of infatuation. It could have been. Francis said *apaixonamento*, which means the same thing, but in his native Galician, something like fascination or a feeling of being bewitched by the other person, or perhaps uncontrolled passion, or some other form of agreed submission, of biocoenosis created from a ray of light. Perhaps it was. Perhaps, too, they were made for each other, like in the romantic novels sold by the sackload from quayside stalls, to be read by faraway sailors or girls awaiting the return of their salty princes, where the lovers seem to be predestined, where impossible love affairs exist between siblings separated by a grim childhood of alienation or migration. Perhaps it was simply a coincidence, fruit of the purest chance, the kind of thing anticipated only by enthusiasts, or those illuminated by the irrational stigma of belief, or even those sitting waiting for love in an enormous auditorium, the ones you hardly ever see any more.

There were no grand words or stereotypical declarations of mutual admiration. There were none because they were superfluous, because their bodies said what words dared not, or could not, or knew not how to express. After all, despite what the physicists or the most timorous rationalists might say, falling in love alters times and coordinates, in such a way that, imperceptibly, as if without realizing it, they began to walk towards the hotel where Rose was staying – the shortest of holidays, a long weekend – more from a studied politeness than a demonstration of the intentions both were nervously concealing beneath an epidermis burning with desire. Simultaneously they offered each other a cigarette, as if there was an astral conjunction or something magic between them, as if they had always known each other or they had powers of divination.

"See you tomorrow," Francis had said with a casualness that came out aggressively and with too sudden a change of rhythm to be sincere.

"You really don't want to come up to my room?" Rose had replied, not recognizing herself in this repeated seizing of the initiative, this laying herself bare to chance, this demolition of blocks and complexes.

"OK. Just for a cigarette and a chat. Tomorrow is Saturday so I do not have to work."

They crossed the hotel threshold furtively, not greeting the receptionist, a Chinese man with a round, bald head who was cradling the bell on his desk, mesmerized by the images on a miniscule television set, where they were showing a repeat of a classic western (Lee Marvin drunk as a skunk, caterwauling the chorus of some ballad).

Up in the room it was all discoveries and revelations, caresses and tenderness. It took them some time to undress, as if they wanted to delay the act itself, but after a thousand kisses in the most accessible places, on lips and cheeks, shoulders and neck, they began to undress one another, slowly, so very slowly, with a burning desire that overflowed from every pore, that was evoked in every movement, that hung like a thick fog in eyes heavy with shared purpose. Francis played with the buttons on Rose's camisole, playfully squeezing the mounds of her breasts while she slid her hand into the crevice that separated his trousers from a belly sculpted by thousands of crunches, where each muscle marked out a field, and there were no curves or discontinuities. Before long, their clothes were falling, piece by piece, to the floor. And now they were naked, San Diego Bay observing them in the distance, stars hanging in a magnificent sky, eyes illuminated by the light like those of a cat poised to pounce. They shifted to the horizontal position, tried out impossible angles and contortions in the gymnastic ecstasy of passion, until they found a position that suited them and that while classic – Rose squatting on her heels and penetrated from beneath – was no less satisfactory for that. Francis reached out in search of Rose's breasts, and she gave herself up to him, arching her back in a contorted spasm. After the first orgasm – gazing hard at one another, sweating their passion, ascending with the sureness of many previous assignments, completely drenched – they went to shower together.

The bathroom was huge with a blinding excess of light. Beneath the stream of water, surrounded by a dense mist, they fell into the relaxed back-and-forth of a happy adult couple, serene in their affection and unhurried, as if certain tonight would last, as if they knew there were not, would never be, any demands or pressures at all.

"I have always liked bathrooms," said Francis as he massaged Rose's back, with a touch of serenity and a great deal of wheatgerm gel.

"I like them too, with all the light and the mirrors, the smell of lavender soap and tropical fruits; the combination is so impossible, but the idea is so exotic."

"Does all that not light bother you?" asked Francis, his eyes half open beneath the curtain of water.

"Sometimes I like to make love in the dark as well, but I prefer the light. I don't know why, but I prefer the light."

"Me too, but not so much of it," said Francis putting his hand in front of his face.

They changed places and then it was Rose who soaped Francis, sliding her lubricated hands over his most intimate areas, moving her palms in ever increasing circles, playfully prodding him with her fingers, scratching with her nails, inventing a relaxation technique or recreating a lesson learned on her own flesh. These massages awakened the desires weakened by the steam from the hot water. They carried out another assault perfumed by the scent of the shower gel and the fragrance of the rose petals that flooded everything, that attached itself to the inside of their noses so neither of them was able to think of anything that wasn't roses and sex, an olfactory association, preconscious and happy. The steam had misted up the mirrors that now just reflected shadows, and it clung to them, making the light even dimmer. They felt the humid passion of the tectonic movement of their bodies – plates shifting over the heat of their internal magma – happy and natural in the perfect combination of senses and flavours, of tensions and the lightest of touches.

They dried themselves on immaculate white towels with the name of the hotel embroidered in relief. They put on the bathrobes, also white and with the hotel monogram on the left breast, and sat down, shooting off intimacies like darts, recovering from the tiredness of their bodies and reinforcing their mutual enchantment. They were soon comfortable, one in front of the other, stretched out in an arc, hips against the seat and leaning on the arms of the sofa, so their connected sexes were the only point of contact. Meanwhile, they gazed at each other like two prone, dead figures; eyes lost and empty, like in a Mantegna painting. Then Francis noticed the coffee maker on the side table, so characteristic of American hotels, and part of the standard equipment at the Hotel Radisson, where Rose had booked in for her weekend in San Diego.

"Coffee?" said Francis as he took a cigarette for himself and leaned forward to offer the pack to Rose.

"That's not a bad idea."

"Where is the coffee? I found the coffee maker, but not the coffee."

"It's all here, sweetheart, in the drawer underneath."

"Oh yeah," agreed Francis, rummaging through the drawer.

"Maybe it'd be better if you made something weak. I have to sleep."

"Didn't you say coffee?"

"Yes, but if there's some decaf it'd be better. I'm tired. If it isn't decaf it'll take me ages to get to sleep. After an hour I'm not tired any more, and then I just can't sleep, however tired I am."

"OK. There is some here. I'll get water from the bathroom," said Francis disappearing and reappearing right away with the coffee jug full of water from the tap.

The conversation lasted through two coffees and four or five cigarettes. They told each other their life stories or, at least, a significant and colourful portion of their life stories. They spoke more of the present than the past, which at times like this always goes by the wayside a little, establishing a tacit silence about the extent of relationships and other commitments.

That had been their first encounter, which benefited from the balm of coincidence, from the complicit darkness of the auditorium, like a spark that had set light to two meandering souls, shipwrecked and rudderless in a vacationing San Diego. Now, in the morning, they continued the conversation in the gardens of Balboa Park, eating Alaska crab and chicken cooked with tofu, drinking Mexican beer and telling each other chapters of their life stories.

Rose had recently been in Ireland, visiting the numerous assorted relatives that any Irish expatriate has on the island. She spoke joyfully and repeatedly of Galway, the city of canals and islands, of the sharp, intermittent, but ever-present rain, of the hundreds of trout and carp ploughing along the river Corrib where there were always Dickensian ruffians, short of stature and skilful in their use of the rod, fishing for carp brought from the nurseries of Asia, where there were always vigorous men in tweed caps, unrestrained beer bellies and elastic-waisted trousers, setting hooks in flight to catch trout in the Eglinton Canal, and elderly retired gentlemen, with arthritic wrists and rhinophymic noses, struggling with the salmon in the currents around Ballyknow Quay. And on and on she talked, with that apparently Celtic passion for speaking of the island as if it were an Edenic paradise, while fleeing from it as if it were a hell of hunger and no prospects. Francis looked at Rose with the wonder of a child blinded by the light in the eyes of a virgin, the darling eyes of a fairy-tale princess, unblinking above a perfect, everlasting smile.

After listening to her – dumbstruck and somewhat disorientated by the lack of sleep – Francis told her anecdotes of his childhood on the outskirts of the Galician town of Padrón, when on summer evenings, which back then seemed infinite, and now so long ago and so sad, they went swimming in the Sar and sailed down the river, in a boat like the ones used for the extraction of sand, until they reached some wells that were called Os Fondóns, because they were so deep, where it was said (mysteries were quite the thing in those days) there lived a monster with seven heads and a dragon's body, with iron scales and a steel sting on the end of his powerful tail. Whenever they went down there – he would never go alone, owing to a prudence that others might call fear – they had to flee the rising current, a maelstrom more imagined than real, dragging them towards the inside of a whirlpool where, it was said, lived the amphibious beast that was going to devour them, one by one, lazily chomping with sharpened, poisonous canines, which, according to another schoolbook mythology, are supposed to be characteristic of such antediluvian creatures. He couldn't really explain why, but, despite the fear, he always went back to the same place, as if drawn there by the songs of the Nereids.

"But that can't be true. You're telling me fibs. You're talking about a made-up world, it's just a collection of tall tales, and not very well put together either," said Rose exchanging her frank smile for a more ambiguous one, somewhere between indignant and amused.

"It might not be true now, but when it happened, when I was a melancholy, anxious child, inhibited and not much of a talker, then it was the only truth."

"Truth? Don't make me laugh", retorted Rose in a tone that unleashed a torrent of fervour from Francis.

"As true as the blackness of the waters where the skeletons of shipwrecks ebbed and flowed with the tide; as true as the darkness of the steps where the water rats would scamper, those chimerical beings, half rat, half fish, who darted across the river, among the layers of leaves embedded in the riverbed, big as rabbits they were, and with sharp pointed teeth like sabres out of a chivalric romance."

"Stop right there, Francis. I believe everything you're saying, but don't keep making things up. It really must have been a terrible childhood," Rose smiled ironically.

"As true, I was saying, as the mussels in the milky sand of the river, the goblins who lived in the hazel trees or the tender, affectionate nymphs who would comb their silvery hair on magical spring nights, just as real as the fox who used to visit my grandfather's fields or the potions the wise old woman of the mill used to make, or…"

"You're a fantasist, the worst kind of pedant and a liar, but you're funny. It doesn't matter if you're telling me the truth or making up stories of fairies and avenging knights, of champions or of mushroom-dwelling dwarves. I don't want to know about your past. It doesn't matter to me."

"Doesn't matter to you?" Francis was slightly annoyed, as if her admission was a highly-evolved form of treason.

"Don't get me wrong. It amuses me, but it doesn't really matter to me. I've got other priorities. What I really want to know is what's going through your mind now. At this moment. What are you thinking?"

"Now?" asked Francis surprised.

"Yes, now. What's going through your mind now? Not when you were a boy, not a year ago, not even yesterday, but now," said Rose with a hint of mystery and a great deal of conviction.

"Lots of sensations. I could not say how many. There's the smell of the tofu mixed up in this chestnut sauce, there's the chatter of those tourists on their way to the zoo, in that perpetual holiday uniform, brandishing their cameras like a battle standard, there's those eyes of yours seeing my confusion and laughing, the feeling of touching the grass where I am sitting, that gentle breeze, like an imperceptible gust from San Diego Bay… What's passing through is not important, Rose. What's important is what stays, what will one day blossom into the archives of memory."

"That's a lot of sensations to process all at once," said Rose getting up from the ground and gesturing towards the gates of the zoo, as if looking for a way out, tired of the conversation. "We could go and visit the zoo. I heard there are some really cute pandas."

"Cute how?" Francis asked ironically.

"Cute like you, if that's what you were hoping to hear. Come on. Let's go."

They got up reluctantly. Beyond the sheltering shade of the brambles where they had been sitting for their own special picnic, there was a sticky heat, a great deal of humidity and little possible respite. A stifling heat, like a slow grilling, constant sweating and heaviness in the legs and breath. They picked up the leftovers and drank the last drops of mango juice from the bottom of the carton.

On the way to the entrance, Francis stripped to the waist, showing off his smooth, muscled chest, the result of early-morning stretches and endless crunches, the cult of the body and a great deal of narcissistic effort.

They paid sixteen dollars a head for some entrance tickets with the logo of the Zoological Society of San Diego: two elephants beneath a tree in the savannah, a snake, and an eagle silhouetted in the branches of the tree. All very epic and very cold, like nouveaux riches sated with material things, but thirsting after heraldic shields, caught up in the most unsettling confusion and anxious to acquire roots and breeding. It was two in the afternoon and they had plenty of time for a complete circuit of the park, which wouldn't close its gates until well after seven.

As they were about to go through the gates there was an incident, a minor one, but which changed the mood entirely. A female guard in a paramilitary uniform (white soldier-style shirt with captain's armbands, blue trousers with a vertical black stripe, name tag on her shirt pocket with a diminutive that was absurd for such a great bulk) stood in Francis's way and told him he had to put on his vest, because they couldn't let him into the park with his chest on display.

They stood to one side as people went through in tightly-knit groups. The guard was watching them mockingly out of the corner of her eye, sure of her superiority and control.

"Well, maybe there's a law," said Rose resignedly.

"A law? What kind of law would that be?" Francis bellowed at Rose in surprise.

"Be a good boy and don't get in a fight over something so small. It's as if you've forgotten where you are. Except for the island of epidermal liberalism up in San Francisco, this is the state of restrictions and neo-conservatism," Rose said firmly.

"Well, they can go fuck themselves in the ass," Francis mumbled as he pulled his vest over his head. "You have only got to look at that woman's great lumbering carcass, like some kind of pinniped. Very appropriate for a zoo. Yes, maybe that is why they chose her as a guard."

"Don't get annoyed. We want to go in and there are rules. Come on, act like a grown-up, even if it's just for a moment. I know it's hard and it doesn't suit you, but make an effort."

Francis smiled as he calmed down slightly. They rejoined the queue, longer now.

"She wouldn't be able to wear a vest. Even the alligators would flee in terror," Francis insisted.

"Come on, sweetheart, don't go on about it," Rose soothed, mollifying him now they were approaching the turnstile.

Rose took Francis by the arm and whispered something in his ear, to avoid an exchange of inappropriate words between Francis and the sea-lion guard, the fishwife guard, the unbending, mastodon-like guard, who had stood in their way with such an inflexible attitude. The guard let them pass but not before looking them up and down just to emphasize the power differential.

The incident resolved – acceptance of inevitability and rules, denial of freedom of dress, pragmatic position of renunciation – they went into the zoo, joining the migratory flow of hundreds of other tourists, all enthusiastic and happy and enjoying their free time.

Although it wasn't easy to push their way through the hordes in the thrall of their zoophilic passion, they eventually came across a sign with a picture of a tiger's head. Without giving it any more thought – they shared a curiosity for deciphering coded messages in the stripes on the big cats' coats – they walked in the direction indicated by the sign. They went down a slope that snaked between dwarf palms and luxuriant vegetation – doubtless a microclimate created by an environmental engineer, who had studied at Harvard or Columbia, to help tropical species adapt to San Diego's mild climate – eventually reaching an area marked out by a ditch and a rail, and supposedly occupied by the fearsome Bengal tigers.

In front of the railings, mountains of people were working their cameras to death and sweating buckets because the damned microclimate was so accurate (tragedies of technique) but dodging and giggling (techniques of tragedy), they managed to create a space among the families of Mexicans and Taiwanese, who seemed to be multiplying like hordes of foul-mouthed ants. The disappointment was huge. The tiger, or the tigress (because there was only one specimen to be seen and the sex wasn't very clear), wasn't moving and didn't even deign to look at the public, a disdain that would make Borges himself pale, lover that he was of tigers and the messages they carry written on their flanks.

They carried on walking, sweating and somewhat cowed by the excessive humidity, and they went from one disappointment to the next. A polar bear decided he didn't want to bathe in the pool in front of his cave into which, despite the official notices, the tourists were throwing all sorts of fruits and treats. Further on, in their tiny cages, some haughty birds avoided being photographed by ostentatiously displaying the damaged behaviour of psychotic animals. Next, some cobras, motionless, supposedly with the intelligence of wily assassins – a paradigm created from ignorance and fear – were huddled against the glass walls of an enormous terrarium, and it was heartbreaking to see them there, swallowed up by the almost empty space and perpetual inaction.

The list of disasters didn't stop with the cobras' terrarium. There was more, a chain of absences and divergences. So there were also stinking tapirs snuffling through their own excrement; neurasthenic macaques, victims of an obsessive passion; unhappy hippopotami in their tiny pool; giraffes with necks rubbed raw by frenetic scratching against the branches of an acacia; panthers with sharpened canines; bulimic orang-utans blackened with scabrous marks; rhinoceroses with mutilated horns; alligators who had lost their ferocity with the change of diet; immobile gazelles, paralyzed by the absence of open spaces; near-blind manatees, their eyes inflamed by the excess of chlorine; albino kangaroos, tendons atrophied from lack of jumping; hyenas who had stopped laughing, who could only cry over their misfortune as caged animals; pangolins with their scales bleached by the deficiencies of their surroundings; androgynous lions; diving lizards, and other aberrations of animal behaviour arising from prolonged and perspective-free captivity, an immaculately planned torture – Dachau farm, Treblinka farm – an omen of a future that would be anathema to standardized hominids, all well trained in following rules and perversely focused on the future.

Francis was beginning to get twitchy from all the mental paralysis and contagious neuroses.

"What the hell are we doing here? I am getting depressed," he said despairingly.

"Calm down a bit. We came to see the pandas. Be a good boy and don't get annoyed. The only one who's suffering is you."

Rose assumed the role of conciliator without much conviction, but she couldn't deny that the idea, the insistence on seeing the pandas, had been hers, like a good little tourist brought up on tourist-office brochures.

"OK. But after the pandas, we are having a change of scene. It's starting to get me down."

Francis set off on a digression about the cruelty of confinement, about the futility of this kind of institution now that technical advances meant you could see the animals in their own environment, on webcams or those great wildlife documentaries. There was no need – no need at all – for such ignoble captivity. What's more, all you'd ever see there was a pale reflection of a panther's elasticity, a false image of a giraffe's gracefulness, a pathetic imitation of a buffalo's power...

Rose, nervous of discovering a negative aspect of Francis that she did not want to explore, cut him off with a playful suggestion.

"Let's go and have an ice cream, and then we'll get straight in line to see the panda cubs. I can't wait!"

"You have to wait in line? Will it be long?" Francis muttered with a distinct lack of enthusiasm.

"Not long. It says it here. On this poster. They allow visitors after four in the afternoon. Just for two hours."

"Two hours?"

"Yes. Two hours. Apparently they're very sensitive animals."

They had no choice but to get in line at the ice-cream kiosk. Two families of Mexicans had monopolized the attention of a single inexpert vendor with massive orders and combinations of flavours that were all but impossible (the combinations, not the flavours). This obstacle overcome, ice creams in hand, they changed line to join the one for the visit to the panda enclosure. To their surprise and discomfort, in the few minutes they had spent buying the ice creams, the line for the pandas had grown so long that they couldn't even see the entrance door.

"Don't worry," said Rose soothingly. "It'll move quickly. They don't let people stay for more than a couple of minutes."

"That's all? Just two minutes and we have to wait like idiots for all these people to go through?"

"Yes. It's like seeing and not seeing. It hardly gives you any time to focus on details, but it's an image that will stay with you for the rest of your life. An image that will always come back to you, like first love and melancholy."

"It's too much. Sixteen dollars to spend two minutes looking at a panda cub. At least melancholy is free."

"Some people like to see the animals and spend the whole day here. We're the weird ones, nothing seems to means anything to us and we spend the whole day complaining about everything," said Rose thoughtfully, with a suggestion of habitual self-criticism.

"Maybe you're right," Francis agreed. "It will be better to get excited about the pandas. To think it's a unique spectacle and all that. Maybe even forget the stifling heat that is making this ice cream melt so damn fast."

"You'll see when they open the door how quickly it'll move," said Rose.

It was true, as soon as they opened the door of the little garden where the pandas were kept, the line began to move rapidly, in fits and starts, in groups of ten or twelve people. The guards followed a well-worn routine. They opened the door, let a set number of people go through and began to time two minutes. When just over a minute and a half had passed they invited those present to have a final look – photos were prohibited – and immediately cleared the way for another group to squeeze in.

When their turn came, with two Taiwanese families at full pitch, talking ceaselessly in their language of rising and falling tonics, Bai Yun, the female panda, offered them an unexpected circus act, somersaulting on the end of a branch and gracefully peeling a bamboo shoot. It was all they managed to see after a half-hour wait, a strawberry ice cream and a leisurely conversation about the panda's thumb and the revealing works of Stephen J. Gould, the king of popular science writing. The experience was positive and worth the wait. It served to concentrate their plans and to construct a magical moment between Francis and Rose, which was certainly worthwhile.

After the panda micro-show – two brief but intense minutes – they weren't in the mood for looking at more neurotic animals. And so they decided to find a seat on a terrace under the shade of an umbrella that would protect them from the sun, to order some drinks and free their neurosis – and this time it would be their own, not the stupid anthropomorphization of animal behaviour – smoking a few cigarettes amid the date palms and wrought-iron cages, where one could imagine dangerous animals sunk in the tedium of endless visits, fearless wild felines and leathery-scaled reptiles, more fitting for a nineteenth-century lunatic asylum than for a zoo at the end of the twentieth century.

Tired as they were of seeing animals caged and hordes of families mechanically repeating the same movements as other hordes of families before them, soon to be automatically followed by ever more disorientated tribes, torn between what they liked to do and what they understood they ought to like to do to fill their free time, regularly confusing free time with consumption, they decided to get back in the blue cabriolet and get out of the zoo as quickly as possible, leaving Balboa Park behind them.

As they weren't in a hurry and had no need to be back anywhere – it was a bit early to eat or to go back to the Radisson – they decided to visit one of the solitary coves just off the road north, on the way to Los Angeles (Ell-Ay, the locals said), out past the town which, in that strange American way, they call La Jolla (actually they pronounce it *la ioia*, but such technicalities don't go down so well over there). They felt free and energized, in love and full of illusions and life. Rose was driving rather too carefully, but better that way, thought Francis, who wasn't in the mood to be jolted about and was willingly doing the job of co-pilot, picking over the secrets of a large-scale road map.

After twenty minutes they saw a sign warning of a *Detour Ahead*. Francis began to sing an arrangement he knew from a Billie Holiday CD (*slow down before you crash and break your heart... Oh lucky me, that suddenly I saw the light... smooth road, no detour ahead...*). They decided it wasn't a bad idea to follow the sign and took the detour. The track – to call it a road would be lexical overkill – led down towards the sea and rounding a curve, they discovered a marvellous place, one of the many that garland the south California coast.

It was a little horseshoe-shaped cove bordered by solid rocks and cliffs that marked the edges of a sandy inlet only visible at the lowest tide. The place was surrounded by acacias and eucalyptus and by a herbaceous carpet permanently damp from the mist that sprayed up from the Pacific. The sun was on its way down and they decided to go down to the sand to watch the sunset. It seemed the most appropriate end to such a romantic evening, with all its certainties and surprises.

From the beach, which stretched out before them for no more than a couple of hundred feet, they could see, in a V-shaped gorge previously hidden from view by acacias, between two rocky walls, a horsetail waterfall some fifty or sixty feet high. The sight left them dumbstruck.

Once over their initial awe they walked for a bit until they reached the foam from the waves that rose one after another up the slope and on to the sand. The greenish-blue sea had changed imperceptibly to a greyish blue. There was a bit of an undertow and they decided not to risk going too far in, staying close instead to where the waves were breaking. The inconvenient absence of light and the isolation of the spot made them especially careful. They splashed around a little and looked for shells with the foolishness of lovers for whom all nature's wonders seem unique and unrepeatable, for their eyes only, a cause for joy and erotic rapprochement. They talked, too, of trivial things – the last play they had seen, the records they had bought the day before, a report in *National Geographic* on Angkor or on whale sharks, a book by Gore Vidal or the two-way relationship between advanced informatics and industrial beauty – perhaps to forget other things, the important ones, the ones that mean hard work and commitment, that inspire fear and anticipate old age. It certainly worked and that's how they felt, more and more invulnerable, like when they were adolescents; or avenging angels of justice, like when they were children; or simply immortal, like they did at that tender age when adults keep children as far away as possible from death.

Francis left the water and started to draw in the sand with a twig, distractedly, as if thinking about something located beyond Rose, beyond the beach, beyond himself. Rose watched him from the water, seeking explanations for his remoteness.

"Do you love me?" Rose asked suddenly, emerging from the water and revealing the full glory of a fine-figured Irishwoman.

"What kind of a question is that?" said Francis, looking her in the eye.

"The kind you don't ask."

"You're right. If you don't know the answer don't ask that sort of question and if you do know the answer then you don't need to ask," said Francis, starting to put on his vest and socks.

"Maybe you're right. Maybe we have very different backgrounds. In Ireland we ask that sort of question. That's what we're like."

"Don't generalize. Don't speak for a whole country. Speak for yourself."

"I am. I asked the question. It might be the kind of question you don't ask, but I asked it."

"We'd best be getting back to San Diego. I'm hungry and it is starting to get cold."

"You're right, Francis. I hadn't realized, but now I can feel the cold of the night."

"Give me a kiss."

"Do you love me?"

"Don't go on about it. Let me keep a bit of discretion, even if it is only with words."

It didn't take them long to dress and climb up to the side of the track where they had left the car. The ride back was silent. An Elis Regina CD and a few words exchanged in praise of past and present landscapes, going back over the day's events and the moments they had shared.

Back in San Diego they found a Japanese restaurant – Rose had a certain preference for what she considered exotic without considering the image she projected to the Japanese, or the Mexicans, or even to Francis, for whom Rose was indubitably exotic – for a light dinner before what they foresaw would be a full-scale carnal assault.

In a shopping centre they found a sushi bar that looked good from the outside. It was still a bit early and there weren't many customers. The waiter approached them solicitously and offered them the menu. Without wasting a second, they ordered Sapporo beer and a soup of the day to start. When the waiter brought the soup, which was sublime, Rose took the initiative and ordered *uni* (sea-urchin eggs), *taco* (octopus), eel and yellow-fin tuna, which came with a skilfully mixed accompaniment of spicy radishes and soy sauce. They rounded off the celebration with a shot of hot sake, which brought on an urge to talk. They were happy lingering over the conversation, drawing up an inventory of shared interests that included Japanese food, hot sake, Sapporo beer and jasmine tea with sugar lumps.

From the restaurant they went straight to the hotel. They were tired and content just to go back over a few intimacies, to mark out territories and expand their mutual knowledge. As they talked, they exchanged languid caresses, desire contained by tiredness.

Francis talked of his previous occupation as a teacher of Hispanic literature, while he was living in Chicago, on the shores of Lake Michigan, of his friendship with Andy, his most loyal friend – he declared – and how difficult it had been for him to adapt to California, of his little house on San Rafael beach and his work for a publishing house in San Francisco.

Rose talked of an abortive relationship, when she was still very young and living in Boston, of how she had moved to California, of her work for an IT consultancy, of her apartment in San Francisco to which, by the way, he had a standing invitation, and of how disappointed she had been about the pandas.

They smoked two cigarettes and drank vast quantities of water to avoid a hangover and flush out their kidneys, so they could carry on talking and clear their heads.

Despite all their predictions, that night they didn't make love.

It was the first weekend they spent together. Later there would be many more, until they had woven a web of meetings and commitments, dependencies, security in routine, all the things that apparently constitute the core of any relationship.

2

It was the beginning of spring. The house was sad, empty of sounds and living beings. Francis had arrived home from the hospital, from finding out his test results. With a routine, automatic movement, comforted by the action and the familiar territory, he connected the hi-fi cable and pressed the *random* button to play an arbitrary mix of tracks from two CDs (Jorge Ben and Margareth Menezes). He stood there in shock, looking out at San Rafael beach. Deaf and in shock. There was music, but Francis wasn't listening. Francis had pressed the button, but Francis was dead. Or rather, Francis wasn't alive.

He went to the bathroom and found the scissors. Those curved scissors, so comfortable and so effective. He began cutting the nails on his left hand, which was easier for him. As he attacked the nails on his right foot, he let out an unsettling cry, as if he were an orphan child who had lost his adoptive parents, as if nobody could silence that wailing that came from deep within, from sadness and rage, from his most intimate and dramatic depths.

An indeterminate period of time passed, it could have been long or short, depending on who was measuring. A time in which Francis was visualizing his future like a countdown. The months would turn into weeks, days, hours, minutes, thousandths of a second on a knife-blade of perception and then nothing, *res*, *rien*, *nada de nada*, ever again, black on black on a black background. He spent a while imagining what would happen to him. He would press on his eyeballs, see a green stain around two red spots, feel his most intimate structures shut down forever, say a final goodbye with an implosion like the one you get when you turn off the TV, and then nothing: *adieu, black will be black forever*. Forever. No remission. The green stain. Turned off. Nothing. Maybe not even dreams.

Suddenly, a phone call brought him back to his current life. Francis was alive and listening to Brazilian music on his hi-fi, looking hopefully at the waves of the Pacific and cutting his nails in the white-and-blue-tiled bathroom. He had the scissors in his hand and didn't know what to do with them, whether to put them on the bidet or keep hold of them. He went to the phone. On the way to the bedside table he put the scissors on a shelf, swallowed his tears and took a deep breath, as if trying to scare off all the obsessions gnawing away at his brain. As if nothing was real but the phone call, the shiver he got hearing the phone ring, the cat skulking with feline rhythm between the bushes in the garden.

On the other end was his publisher, Martin, the one who assigned him the urgent translation jobs, which put food on the table, but also brought out his chronic anxiety, like a Pavlovian rat or a kitten injected with alkaloids.

Martin was talking in a rush, like he was anxious or nervous, or something had disturbed him terribly. No. Straight away. No. It couldn't wait until tomorrow. The project he had on his desk was an absolute priority. Absolute. Did he understand? Absolute. And he insisted again and again that as far as he was concerned there was only a single meaning of the word *absolute*, he wouldn't admit any other meaning.

Francis tried to get him to settle down a bit and talk calmly about the reason for the call. He tried, with no joy, to get him to focus on the subject and talk about it on the phone, to be more explicit and less ambiguous. Impossible. No. We'll talk in the office. Don't keep on. It's not the kind of thing you can talk about on the phone. The phone is for other things, for the messages and sweet nothings of the first days of romance, for locating somebody or leaving messages, not for discussing work projects. Goodbye. Martin had hung up, categorically and impetuously pressing the button that disconnected his mobile phone.

Martin almost always behaved violently by phone, as if he hated having to talk at a distance. If he wanted to make contact he would leave a message; he insisted on talking about everything in private, face to face, as if he barely considered the phone an appropriate medium for business. He wouldn't get into discussions or give explanations. It was a philosophy shared by many people in the publishing world, they didn't have much confidence in long-distance deals, and they considered the phone an instrument for lies. Fine if you're the one who has to lie, but terrible for deals and negotiations.

Martin wanted to have his interlocutor in front of him, whoever it was, to analyze gaze and movement, to be able to capture the weakness in every nervous response, from an excess of sweat on the forehead to a light dryness on the lips and in the mouth, from excessive gesticulation to a tendency to look away when talking, so typical of those unsure of themselves or tormented by some socially unacceptable difference.

His philosophy of work and the negotiation of business conditions was very simple. Talk about things face to face and then, straight away, agreements written down in a document and signed at the bottom, in duplicate, as one must in these times of lawyers and mistrust, of the denial of any ethical commitment and so much treacherous competition. He had been in business for many years and learned many lessons that evinced the uselessness of altruism in any part of life.

After the news from the hospital, Francis wasn't in the mood to be rushed, but work was work and his work situation was too complicated to turn down a commission. These people lifted you to the top or dropped you to the bottom with terrifying ease. He would have to work like a demon and save like an ant for when there was nothing. He would have to get in the car and go to the publisher's office in San Francisco, to see what could be such a priority, so urgent and so secret to get Martin in such a state. It would almost certainly be a last-minute translation, for a conference on Neurology or Genetics, Botany or Cultural Anthropology, some foreign researcher who wanted to present a paper or give a speech and who required somebody else to revise his unacademic English stuffed full of neologisms and unsuitable constructions, so typical of the immigrant brain and its uncertain syntax.

The tears he had shed before the phone call, so apparently decisive and yet barely consoling, the uncontrolled weeping and shaking, had given way to an agitated inaction, in which Francis was debating with himself, unsure what to do, who to ask for help or advice, which way to turn at this crossroads where the paths forked, intersected, became entangled. There were various options but his mind was moving as slowly as the most lethargic tortoise. He could pick up the telephone and make some therapeutic calls to his girlfriend, to his friend Andy who lived in Chicago, but was always there when he was needed. No. And Rose? How would he tell Rose? Impossible. Impossible to do it by phone, not to mention barely courteous given that she was the woman with whom he was aiming for – or at least she was convinced they were aiming for – bigger and more solid commitments, a home and a couple of kids chasing butterflies in the garden, dogs and mortgages, holidays on some third-world beach or at a fashionable ski resort. And what about Andy? He couldn't tell Andy either. It definitely wasn't the easiest moment to tell him something as serious as that, the poor guy was going through a depression, after his mother's death. Better to take the car keys – always left where you least expect them – turn off the hi-fi and close the patio doors.

Francis was in a trance, as if possessed by a magnetic force that was pinning him down, thinking with his eyes wide open, his gaze reflected in a concave mirror, all astonishment or fear. He shrank into himself. A samba or a bossa nova was playing, hardly appropriate for his state of mind, or maybe it was the best alchemy, highly protean and liberating, the fog where he could hide from his misery and fear.

By the time the convertible pulled out on to the beach road, Francis was in another world. In this narrowing funnel, becoming darker and less familiar, he was moving automatically and mentally relaxed. His mind allowed the countryside to pass by unobserved, without storing it in the electronic labyrinths of his glial cells, concentrating exclusively on its most recent obsession: illness. An illness without a name. Without a label. Without an identified cause. That would leave him blind. Lost to the world and blind. Like a mole. Like an albino cave lizard. Like an eyeless fish dwelling in karstic labyrinths.

How could he tell his lifelong friends, his girlfriend with all her plans? How could he tell any of them, without disintegrating like a sandcastle, that he was ill, sentenced to death, irretrievably condemned? How to deal with it? How not to give up? How not to feel the curse of Juno? How not to succumb to madness like Oedipus, tearing out his own eyes, for their uselessness, defectiveness, sinfulness? How not to feel he was an unfortunate Atlas condemned to a lifetime of supporting a world that isn't, that escapes, viscous, from between his hands?

He mentally picked over the crust of reality, playing out scenes of clandestine meetings and pathetic declarations, enormous silences and vigorous, tragic reactions. Why now, just when he had a girlfriend and a job, projects and a life? Why him? What had he done, God, what had he missed? Questions he had always said he would never ask, which seemed absurd and ridiculous, a denial of probability and chance, but which welled up, automatically, after the first moments of bewilderment and incredulity, of blushing and wandering around, a soul in torment touched by the gods.

He had found out days ago, just by chance during a routine medical check, about the problem with his eyes. "A degenerative condition of the retina," the doctor had said, "a very rare condition we don't know the origin of and have no cure for. Possibly a virus, but we're not sure – and nor, of course, is the treatment."

Just like that, so blunt and cold, such a clear-cut prognosis and so little hope, as out of place as a hedgehog on a silk sheet, as if losing your sight was something banal and unimportant, inane and not at all tragic, something that can happen every day and therefore shouldn't really affect us.

"Six months from now you'll be completely blind. There's no cure. It's all I can tell you. There's no known cure."

Not even a *yet*, which could suggest a possible solution, or open a miniscule window to a ray of confidence, a bridge leading to a way back, an environment that could become bearable through self-deception, a mirror image to give the lie to an appearance of truth. Nothing. Not even a possibility. A clear sentence, like a barber's blade, dissection and rupture, cold lightning.

At the start there had been only defensive and self-interested incredulity, essential if he was to go on living, to stop the hand of destiny, to withdraw into himself and think about a future in chiaroscuro, in filmic fusion leading to the terrifying blackness of optical oblivion. He still hadn't noticed any symptoms, except – perhaps this was the first symptom – a discreet photophobia which he had initially interpreted – erroneously, he sensed now – as a passing allergic reaction to the spring sunlight, which is apparently very malign and which always appears without warning, sudden and intense, like cancer and melancholy.

How stupid! he thought. There wasn't even the faintest hint of spring sunshine over there. He was still thinking in terms of what in Europe they call the continental or Atlantic climate, so clear about the seasons and their sequence. Now he lived in California, the Golden State, where the sun was always shining – in real life and in the songs – and where there were rarely surprises in the changing of the seasons, but instead a continuity without surprises, like weather designed not to inconvenience you, to allow you to live a slow, easy life, carefree and soft, a life of pleasure and contemplation.

In the beginning had been incredulity and doubt about the diagnosis, reinforced, obviously, by the absence of any serious symptoms and by his hesitation to believe in doctors as the shamans of a foreign, reactionary culture, and especially in what they say, a magical and hermetic language, far from reality. "It must be a mistake," he repeated mechanically until he arrived at a spiritual state of scepticism, of incredulity, of substitution by a single idea, of sectarian blindness that wants to see nothing outside the Cartesian universe, miserably Euclidean and inflexible, reductionist and profoundly pathetic.

Then, and without a perceptible shift, he had reached desperation, terrible disconsolate weeping, the constantly-repeated vision of an imperfect future of strange silences – the sound of claws and joints, the itching of bugs behind his eye sockets, physical pain in the swollen hollows, the vast impotence of a dismasted ship, of a skinned animal, a trunk eaten up by fungi, asphyxiated by ivies, rotted by the plague of termites, dried out by the chemical death of its roots – of being condemned to the absence of known stimuli.

Now, after a period of ambivalence, his soul fluctuating constantly between the most childish and ingenuous incredulity and the least balanced and not at all reflective desperation, everything was different. There was a tacit formal acceptance, ambiguous resignation and a degree of scepticism about the prognosis. Francis was driving his convertible along the coast road, from San Rafael to San Francisco. A light breeze came up from the sea, too soft to make him put the hood up, and it brought him memories of journeys and romances, of marvellous visions and epic reflections, astonished gazes and pleasures that entered through the eyes before being tested through touch, the tips of his fingers travelling across an entire body; through smell, sniffing the secretions that moistened the most intimate corners; through taste, his taste buds sampling the sweetness of nipples and the saltiness of hips, the acidity of armpits and the bitterness of the unrepentant smoker's lips; through hearing, lovers murmuring an interminable series of huge words – *Je t'aime / I love you / Gosto de ti / Ti amo* – of promises made to be broken – *Toujours / Para sempre / Forever, ever, ever... my love* – of betrayals of reason and feeling, of whispers and sobs – *Mon amour / My love / Cuore / Carissimo* – that weren't always sincere or well judged.

On the beach some lads were floating on their surfboards, elastic as angels or contortionists. For them life seemed a forgiving place, where everything was waves and sea, beaches and sand, physical fitness and lots of sex. Lots of sun. Lots of beach. Not too much love and plenty of sex, which always have been and always will be different things, with clear boundaries and agreed rituals. A soft and relaxed life, without a doubt. An ambiguous indolence. A lifestyle to explore, to invent and reinvent each day, with more twists and turns than Francis could imagine, anchored in the Cartesian rationalism of a man at ease in the system.

He, Francis, also lived a tranquil and harmonious life. A good job at the publishing house where he worked as a translator and, sometimes, even as an editor, compiling texts or looking after the technical aspects of the edition. He had found a nice and very affectionate girlfriend, who looked after him and made him really happy. He had some magnificent friends, the sort who never let you down and are always around when you need them, as faithful and loyal as could be, firm, constant, sure, sensible and discreet.

He too had a forgiving and relaxed life, like those lads who went sometimes surfing and sometimes swimming and enjoyed a fabulous lifestyle, mostly sitting on the sand, watching the waves come and go, dreaming of a world that floated around them, in their universe of marijuana and no worries, sunbathing for countless hours, innumerable days, forever.

He thought that if you looked at it closely, his whole life had been a perpetual holiday. Family. Studies. Travel. Love. All perfect or nearly perfect, exceeding the most optimistic expectations of a boy born at the end of the earth. A loving family, somewhat reticent when it came to talking about problems, but where everything happened with a tacit order, without overstatement or drama. Happy schooldays, camaraderie and lots of shared secrets. Some magnificent travels, whether solitary as a wolf on the steppes or in the best possible company. And love affairs, few but well structured, full of discoveries and rediscoveries, experimentation and change. No. His life had never been, and wasn't now, any worse than that of those boys who went straight from the cradle to the skateboard and from school to the surfboard, and from there, with whatever the judge decided in their parents' divorce and a part-time job in a pizzeria or a workshop, to university, or to travel the world in search of waves, from Hawaii to Tarifa, Australia to the Maldives, with no responsibility other than to be young and to stretch out their youth as long as possible, with no aim other than to be famous and committed activists, archangelic ecologists, defenders of filmable utopias, and artists as well, dreamers of marine gargoyles, of amphibious men and chimerical animals and curly-haired boys stretched out on the foam.

That damned illness with no precise definition – "a very rare condition we don't know the origin of and have no cure for. Possibly a virus, but we're not sure" – had come to destroy all that harmony, all that tranquillity, all that calm, real or imagined. Perhaps one of those lads also had a serious health problem. Something that would sentence him to life in a wheelchair or being plugged into a respirator – like a vegetable, the old folk would say, keen as darts in their careful cruelty, precise as kingfishers swooping in for food, certain in their terrible diagnosis, almost always right in their evaluation of the final consequences – or to dying slowly from an expansive metastatic cancer. Something terrible, signifying a definitive outcome, no way back, permanent disability and a life dependent on others, blinded forever to the pleasure of free will.

Life was like that, merciless with established plans, as unpredictable in its duration as in its circumstances, terribly determinist and, at the same time, guided by fate, by what can't be controlled, by what makes men so vulnerable and so rarely masters of themselves and their destiny.

The area where in the past there had been fields of figs and oranges, on what the Americans called the Peninsula, had since 1970 developed into an industrial community based on the most advanced information technology. That was where Rose worked, caught up in endless programming sessions, in tedious meetings where everybody was the manager of something, of the unit or the sector, marketing or finance, programming or personnel. He thought about Rose, about how he would tell her what he could no longer keep to himself, about what was going to be a gash in their relationship, in their future, now so imperfect, an ex-future, with so few possibilities. That was when he drove on to the Golden Gate Bridge, the city's favourite picture postcard since it was built in 1933, a marvel of technique and engineering, emerging from the ubiquitous fog, so characteristic of San Francisco's microclimate, which seemed to produce a permanent mist, clutching to its heart every cloud that came in off the Pacific.

He thought about Rose, about blindness, sun, photophobia, the doctor's cruelty, the surfers, Rose again, and carried on driving across the bridge, which seemed to float in the mist, as on so many days in that tranquil, liberal, half-European and almost perfect city that was San Francisco.

3

He was thinking about all this – the sun, the photophobia, the incredulity, the doctor's unmitigated cruelty, Martin's phone call, the surfers, the urgent translations, fate, if such a thing exists, his girlfriend, Rose, his possible future, friends, Andy, especially Andy, embodiment of ex-futures shut off once and for all – when he reached the door to the publisher's office.

He took the stairs two by two up to the first floor. The stairs to the second floor, he took more slowly and with less energy. The years had not passed in vain and since he left Chicago he had broken off all contact with the gym. He would have to start exercising again. He needed it. He could feel it. It was down to laziness and lack of incentive. With Andy it was different. Andy encouraged him to look after himself, to smoke less, to drink little or nothing, to exercise, to wear aftershave – Banana Republic, his favourite – to think about his choice of clothes and shoes, to pay attention to himself and his body, to take his antioxidant pills every morning, the right amount of fibre, his daily fruit and vegetables and all that. Rose was different, perhaps for her he tried to take care of his dress and his appearance, but when it came to the rest of it she was more Irish and decidedly anarchist, drinking was good and healthy, smoking a pleasure and it didn't matter whether you ate lobster or octopus, what counted was eating and looking good.

He was totally at ease as he went into the office, greeting everybody with the appearance of a contagious and enduring good mood. Some apprenticeships prepare you magnificently for every occasion, for weddings and funerals, for a job interview with some balding jerk who thinks he's better than you because he has two master's degrees from Harvard and a few words of French (you speak Portuguese, a little Romanian and Dutch and a few words of Arabic, but this doesn't interest him, it isn't a master's degree from Harvard and so it means nothing), or for a cocktail party at a European embassy, soused in French wine of indefinite origin and some minute portions of absurd canapés, which are trying to pass for beluga caviar, but turn out to be lumpfish eggs dyed in squid ink or a toxic aniline that could destroy your kidneys without you realizing it, or at the presentation of a book by some fashionable author, easy prose for lazy romantics, or for illiterate idiots of either sex who have fallen in love with the author photo, with its angelic face or protective presence, depending on the circumstance. Some apprenticeships serve to get you in and out of anywhere, as if you were on your own turf. At the best and worst moments. There are always mirrors which deform, whose distorting image models or conceals the most miserable and least presentable reality, or which alter even our own self-perception. And if there are none, we invent them, concave or convex, full-length or half-length, it doesn't matter, but mirrors that deform, miracles of light and the fantasy of opposites.

"Martin, the director, is expecting you," the secretary announced automatically and respectfully as she foraged away in her computer, where she seemed to swim with the passion of a dolphin saved from the nets of a giant trawler.

Martin called him in over the intercom, briskly and with no concession to his secretary with her ecological hobbies, stupidity and other deficiencies, both physical (despite repeated surgery on her gigantic breasts and hips), and psychological (that flaky mystical-naturalist tendency that is so common throughout California, destroying lives and presaging millenarian catastrophes).

Martin was against dolphins. He said people should eat them, that anything that comes from the sea is edible. In this he seemed not Anglo-Saxon but Chinese; it was a phrase he repeated often, "everything that comes from the sea is edible," to which ever since he had detected his secretary's pro-dolphin stance, he now added, "even dolphins." Martin had recently read an article by Natalie Angier, a science journalist who published portentous essays in *The New York Times*, saying dolphins are highly cruel and savage, that they carry out rapes on the females of other schools, collectively violate kidnapped females and abandon the babies after their mothers have given birth. Since then nobody had managed to get him to shed a tear – not a single one – for a dolphin or a whale. He had passed from one radicalism to another, as so often happens in life.

Francis had barely got through the door when his hand was grasped in an automatic ritual of greeting and declaration of good intentions, and Martin began to talk right away, leaving no time for preambles or social rituals, with the passion of a chronic psychopath afraid of silence. Of silence and formalities.

Francis expected this and sat down without ceremony and without waiting for Martin's invitation – he knew from experience that Martin wouldn't stand to greet him, that after the squeeze of hands he wouldn't invite him to sit down or offer him a coffee or let him get a word in edgeways until he'd got out everything he was storing up inside, so he lit a cigarette, also without waiting for permission, and enjoyed the blue smoke that wheeled and pirouetted around him. Martin was smoking as well and although he had been trying to give up recently – abusive propaganda in the media by those for whom tobacco was the source of all evil, some kind of satanic creation or vengeful recourse of Beelzebub, but also family pressure from his youngest children and from the company, which had a clear anti-smoking policy, reasons of conscience, social pressure and, ultimately, the unequivocal pressure of his own body which demanded to be looked after – he was in solidarity with smokers.

There was a Portuguese writer who was almost certainly going to get the Nobel Prize. That was the core of his speech, which came across to Francis as verbal diarrhoea, with chaotic, complicated syntax, rapid gestures and a great deal of unresolved agitation. If it wasn't this year it would be next year or the one after or the one after that. It wasn't quite clear if this was guesswork or a piece of information acquired through the tortuous channels of intellectual diplomacy. The fact was that Martin was utterly convinced of his premonition / assertion / prediction, and he said so vehemently, his words charged more with conviction than with reason.

Once he had got it all out, he seemed to take a moment, lit the cigarette he had taken from the packet through contagion, through association of ideas, automatically, as when bombs explode out of sympathy, instantaneously and impulsively, with the pure drive of a trapped animal and scarcely of their own volition. Then he began to speak again. This writer, by the name of Saramago, had been named for several years on an unofficial list of possible winners. There were so many petitions and expressions of support, so many translations into Swedish and French, Japanese and Russian, that it was unstoppable. It was an irreversible process. He was sure.

The precise issue – and now the speech was winding down – was that this same writer had recently published a novel, which was already a success on the international market. It had awoken an interest unprecedented for a Portuguese writer, given as they are to a leaden, overcomplicated and none too lucid style. At the Frankfurt Book Fair, the great European shop window for books, the market for the buying and selling of authorial rights, the publishing heart of Europe, various publishers – German, French, Spanish and even Romanian – had bid for the novel and his publishing house had managed, not without effort and with the provision of rather too much money for a writer who was still considered a minority author in the Anglo-Saxon world, to gain exclusive rights for the translation into English of his most recent work to date, *Ensaio sobre a Cegueira* or *Essay on Blindness*. The English edition couldn't wait. He had thought of Francis for the job. He was the best translator they had on the books and he couldn't let them down.

Francis wrinkled his brow indicating that he was going to make a foray into this conversation that had turned into a monologue. Martin didn't give him much choice. He knew very well he was busy with other projects, he said, but this was an absolute priority. No possible delays or postponements. Now. Right now. As soon as possible. They had to get the book on sale in record time. He knew it was a pain and even a rather disagreeable plan. He couldn't let them down now. He owed Martin lots of favours, from when he had arrived in California and didn't have a job, from when they advanced him payments to get him out of a financial hole. From way back when. Lots of favours. Now was the time to call in those favours. He couldn't let them down now. He'd taken a personal gamble. It was time to play for his place.

Francis felt uncomfortable with all this pressure. He liked slow and steady work and planning, knowing in advance when he would have his vacation and how much time he had to do his research. He shifted in his chair and stubbed out his cigarette; he tried to speak but couldn't, thinking to himself and, of course, explaining to Martin what Martin already knew. A translation was not simply the word-for-word transposition of a literary text. You had to familiarize yourself with the author, with his lexicography, with his syntax and his suspended rhythms, like a larva or imago, a Panzer beetle or a writer with a rock in his head, an endogamous insect or a parthenogenetic or polymorphous monster. You had to put a lot of work in first to learn about it all and orientate yourself. That could only happen with experience and a great deal of effort, endless days and lots of going without. The writer turned into an obsession, an insane passion or a figure of irrational hatred, with a little altar at the front door or a target to shoot him in one eye or in the middle of his forehead, in the slit of his mouth or in his heart.

Francis paused to gather energy and Martin seized the conversation. It hadn't always been like that, Martin insisted, at least on the early jobs. Back then it was more about routine and less about feeling, maybe due to the anxiety of youth and the imminent need of a salary, and his translations hadn't been all that professional, not to be too offensive about it. Now it was different. He had a well-earned professional responsibility to his publisher and his readers, out of respect for the writer and respect for himself...

Francis agreed, flattered by the excessive praise that almost made him give in, but he had decided. He couldn't be doing with improvisation and unwanted pressure.

He thought about the surfers, the beach, Rose, Andy, that damned doctor, the translation, the beach again and the surfers, the waves and his illness. He looked at Martin and the fear passed. Martin was expecting a quick and enthusiastic response, words flying like darts, like a teenager about to go out and devour the world. Francis was trapped, he had to leave the parade of images and start negotiating the terms of the job. He had to drag himself out of the slough. By any means possible. The illness didn't exist except in the tortured mind of the oculist. He still hadn't noticed anything special about his eyes. He had even begun to disbelieve what the oculist had told him, out of spite and fear, self-defence and denial of reality. He had to put all those thoughts to one side and concentrate his resources on the job. On the job and on Rose, with no other priorities. He wasn't ill. Or even tired.

He looked at Martin and began to talk about numbers and time, about limitations and handing other commissions to colleagues, about commitments and money, lots of money and about urgent needs, trips, interviews, bonuses and other stipends.

The conversation was fluid and impersonal, generic and without much focus. Martin had read the reviews of the novel in Spanish and French newspapers and was sure it would be a success, not because of the novel in itself, he said – he certainly liked its basic idea very much, although it was no better or worse than many others he had read that year – but rather because of the imminent – and he stressed that word – award of the Nobel. It was a slam dunk. The Portuguese couldn't wait any longer without a mutiny (an intellectual mutiny, of course). They occupied a very important place in the list of the world's most spoken languages and theirs was a very important literature, with a great deal of history and a great many works. What's more, it would have to go to Portugal first of all, to the metropolis where everything had begun, in that kingdom separated from Galicia and Castile in the battles that forged the Iberian Reconquest. In Brazil there were more writers, and better ones, perhaps, but the Swedish Academy was an Academy for a reason and Jorge Amado, the great man of Brazilian letters, the poet from Salvador da Bahia, would have to wait for time to pass and perhaps he would die without the honour of an award that would give him his place on the writers' Olympus, which he deserved as much as Saramago. They were political choices and the Academy, like every academy in the world, was conservative by vocation and in practice. The award of the Nobel to a Portuguese writer would force a change in the public's habits; they would begin to demand the works of this all-but-unknown writer who had been given the prize to beat all prizes.

The novel was too serious to be a publishing success in the Anglo-Saxon world, which tended more towards minor works prefabricated in the best-seller laboratories, designed to be adapted immediately for the big screen, a fevered process based on industrial demand and a lack of literary substance. People wanted action and base passions, not parables and philosophy. But there were also a large number of readers who only read the Nobel or Pulitzer winners, a sort of preselected product, or if they didn't read the books, at least they bought them, which was what mattered to such people, possession of a library well stocked with prestigious names, to impress visitors with. Typical nouveaux riches, drinking their tea with little cucumber sandwiches, the emerging classes where the only residue of culture was the money accumulated in a thousand fraudulent transactions, sales of cattle or baseball players, houses up for auction or land miraculously reclassified by means of a substantial percentage to council employees, and the craving for power, omnipresent and omnimodal, the size of the pool in the garden, or the name of the college where the children would be spoiled rotten. Success was founded on the part of the population with the greatest purchasing power and fewest cares at the point of purchase, to whom you had to give everything pre-chewed and ready-made, who couldn't explore for themselves, but were guided by presenters on the most important TV channels (the vital cradle of literary benevolence), by the best-seller lists (what sold most was good by definition) and by the accumulated prizes (if it won a prize it must be good), who purchased a great many books and read rather fewer of them.

According to commentators – to call some of them literary critics was to do them an unwarranted favour – said Martin, repeating himself, the novel was a parable, a type of literature that wasn't too common, a subtle and at the same time raw reflection on contemporary society, its collective insanities and dehumanizing limitations. It spoke too of the human capacity to inflict pain on our fellow beings. The original was called *Ensaio sobre a Cegueira* and they had to hurry. It would have to be ready for publication when they distributed the new books at the beginning of the autumn. It was a commitment that the whole editorial board had in its sights.

They couldn't afford to make a mistake. That had already happened with a couple of authors, with Kenzaburo Oe and somebody called Cela, and it had been embarrassing. They were a market-leading publishing house and they had to be ahead of the awarding of prizes, foresee everything, even if that meant having to gently probe the members of the Swedish Academy and the Nobel Foundation, since nobody was so innocent these days as to believe financial interests played no part in the dispensation of these prestigious awards.

Prestige was power and power wasn't shared out in handfuls with just anybody. Everything was measured, agreed and calculated beforehand, to satisfy capital. If they could give a Nobel to Kissinger – dear God! – member of a cabinet of imperialists who had supported the filthiest military dictatorships, or Arafat, a terrorist, defender of armed conflict with the Jews, then you could hardly expect a reputation for purity and clarity, altruism and the desire for justice, from that tarnished institution. How could they have let Borges die, blind and weak, without receiving the prize? Why not Lezama, an alchemist of words? Why not Cortázar, a world in himself?

Francis didn't try to counter the arguments, tell him the Nobel Peace Prize was given by the Norwegian Academy, not the Swedish one, since these things didn't go down well with bosses, who consider themselves infallible possessors of reason. Besides, he basically agreed with the political rather than literary character of the prize. As a result, after this disquisition from Martin, who had a natural inclination for South American novelists over the chauvinistic Anglo-Saxons, the conversation veered in a businesslike direction, with Francis pushing as hard as he could, that strategy of asking for more than you expect, in order to get what is at the limit of dignity. Francis said six months and two interviews with the author, to go over the problems and find solutions, to penetrate his most intimate universe, and to do a job he could feel satisfied with. Martin offered three months and the author's address, to write as many letters as they liked, but with no chance of visits, which were very expensive.

In the end, after several coffees and a few more cigarettes than usual, they agreed on four months and one visit before the submission of the first proofs, to solve any remaining queries.

The handshake sealed the agreement while Martin asked the secretary to prepare the contracts, which they would send as soon as possible, signed by the publishing house, for him to sign them as well, keep a copy and send the other to the publisher's office.

They said goodbye in the foyer, under the watchful eye of the dolphin-defending secretary. They had talked of everything, everything except for Francis's imminent blindness.

4

As he left the publisher's – a stifling heat for the season, little or no wind, 100 degrees Fahrenheit, which even made the TV news – Francis was thinking about his situation, going over it again and again in a mind tortured by events. They had come to an agreement. He couldn't turn down the financial offer or the prestige this translation would bring him. If all went well – which it would, it had to, it was high time he had some success – it would be a turning point in his career. No more servitude. No more accepting every single job, however awful. From this moment on he would set the conditions, choose the texts. He was quite certain of that. He would specialize in the writers he liked the most: Sarduy, Lezama and Carpentier, from Cuban Spanish; Piñon, Amado and Lispector, from Brazilian Portuguese; he could publish his own science fiction stories, and if all went well – it had to, it would – it would be their turn to call him and he would be fought over by the best publishers.

He felt himself succumbing to this modern version of *Cinderella* or *The Ugly Duckling*, going over all sorts of fantasies in his head, until he opened the cabriolet door. Getting into the car was always a change of state, from awake to asleep or vice versa, but always with catastrophe and fresh disorder. Pure thermodynamics.

As soon as he grasped the steering wheel – sweating like a condemned man in a galley – he woke up to reality. It occurred to him that this was very possibly his last-ever translation. Six months to go blind and four, at the most, for there were always delays, to finish the translation of *Ensaio sobre a Cegueira*. There would be no afterwards. He would translate that book and it would be the last one he would ever do using the information he got from his sense of sight. No more translations or reading for himself. He would have to learn the reading system for the blind, or repeat old man Opoton's litany: "I am twenty times four years old and I can scarcely see but with my fingers, with the tips of my fingers," or, more tragically, listen to those modern versions of books read out slowly by the text's author, or an actor, or several actors. He was driving like a lunatic along the beach road and daydreaming about blindness, with a funnel of light that was gradually narrowing until everything went black and horrible, like in a dank wolf's den or a weasel's underground burrow. It was a persistent, disturbing thought. So much so that it made him stop the car and get out for some fresh air.

He left the window open to listen to the music, a compilation of the best of Cuban Son. It calmed him right down. It gave him strength and pneumatic joy, as if he was enveloped in a cloud of marijuana or some perverse entropy. He lit up a cigarette as he gazed out at the beach. The waves. The vast ocean. The whale spouts rising imposingly two miles from the coast. The surfers. The sun dancing behind some clouds, their presence so unlikely in that weather, with its stifling heat, its wind. Unreal clouds, like a mirage or an internal tsunami. The waves. The whales. The stifling heat. The surfers. The sunny California coast. His illness. Finishing his cigarette. Chucking away the dog-end. Getting back in the car. Looking at the waves. Thinking about the future. Dreaming about the future. Changing the cassette over. Putting on something by Jobim. Feeling better. Revving up silently, calmly. Pulling out on to the highway. Thinking about Rose. Thinking about Andy. About the whales in the North Atlantic, so close to home. Thinking about going back there. Thinking about the future. Carrying on down the main highway. Reaching a roundabout. Getting off the main highway. Thinking about Rose. Thinking about the squirrels in Lincoln Park in Chicago, about the icy wind that sweeps into the city off Lake Michigan. Thinking about Andy. Feeling better. Dreaming without realizing everything is a dream. Dreaming about getting to the beach house. San Rafael. California.

He turned off the highway unable to stop himself going over and over all the thoughts that were occupying him, hindering him, filling his mind. Automatically, confused, uncontrolled, as if guided by somebody beyond himself, he left the main highway and drove towards downtown. Like all the towns on the California coast, it wasn't very clear where this town began and where its borders with other towns were, but at least the centres were recognizable. Not the historic centres, which either didn't exist or were dilapidated and barely noticeable, in a country with so little urban tradition. The centre was a collection of functional-looking buildings housing four banks and some insurance companies, along with lots of designer shops and the headquarters of several newspapers: the financial heart of the city. The centripetal force that attracts tourists and suburbanites. The force that attracts chancers, immigrants dreaming of a better world, those who didn't dream but had no other choice, the vagrants, those who had so little they no longer even begged, certain that nobody would turn around and help them.

He parked the convertible as best he could and walked slowly towards a branch of Borders, one of the most important book chains in the country, from Seattle to Miami, from New York to San Francisco, with thousands of CDs and books on its shelves, hundreds of customers desperate to buy, buy, buy until their credit cards gave off smoke.

Before going in he decided to allow himself the satisfaction of a fresh cigarette. You couldn't smoke inside. It was strictly prohibited in public places – not counting parks and other open spaces, like the desert or the beach – with an inflexibility that had seemed excessive to him from the first day he set foot in the country, but which he now bore with pragmatic stoicism. As he smoked, he was thinking about what he had to do. Find the author's bibliography and some Portuguese music to give the job a bit of atmosphere. It was a habit of his, one he had picked up through experience and the difficulties of his chosen career. For studying, for writing, even for concentrating, it was good to have a cushion of music to sink into. The art was in selecting the music carefully. Not too strident, nor completely soporific. A cigarette felt so good when you were at your most alert, when you had to measure every step, every action, every movement!

Once inside, in the international literature section, he managed to find some of the things he was looking for. First he went through some new-books catalogues to see if there was any indication of the author's works being published in English. Negative result. His name didn't appear at all in the catalogues of the country's principal publishers. He was soon tired of searching up and down the lists.

He went up to the counter where a blond guy in designer glasses was talking to himself in front of a computer screen. He addressed him carefully, to make sure he was perfectly understood. He couldn't hide his accent. He had been in the country for ten years, but he still had his accent, so very un-Anglo-Saxon. The blond guy put on a business face, which is what you say in these cases, whatever the business might be. He said, why didn't Francis look harder through the catalogues, he had enough to do without having to search for some unknown Portuguese author. This was a books and music superstore, not a specialist bookshop for minority authors. Anyway, he didn't know any Portuguese authors, not that one or any others, so it was most likely they didn't have any at all. If he wanted a book by Tom Wolfe or Norman Mailer, he could tell him right away where he'd find them, but don't talk to him about some Portuguese writer, he had other things to do.

He left the assistant with the words on his lips and went towards another counter where a smiling African

American girl had no hesitation in serving him properly, carrying out a systematic search on the computer. The girl easily managed to find *The Year of the Death of Ricardo Reis*, which had been awarded the Portuguese PEN Club prize and, more importantly when it came to being able to get hold of it there, Britain's famous Independent Foreign Fiction Award. She also found in an online catalogue *The Stone Raft*, a gorgeous book – perhaps another parable – of fantastic criticism in which the Iberian Peninsula breaks off from the rest of Europe and floats across the Atlantic Ocean in search of its African and Latin American foundations.

Francis was satisfied. They were a pair of gems that he'd heard a lot about from his Portuguese friends. Two books essential for getting himself into the universe of that difficult and, sometimes, unfathomable author, always committed to humanity and its liberation, whatever that might mean; betrayal of history or dreamed-of destiny.

The girl asked if he wanted her to keep looking. For now he had enough, Francis confessed. The assistant noted down the reference numbers and promised him she'd be back shortly. Francis entertained himself flicking through a catalogue of art books. Barely ten minutes had passed when the assistant was back with the books. Francis paid with his credit card and politely said goodbye to the girl who had looked after him so well. He thought that perhaps she had treated him better because he was an immigrant, something he put up with, but which never ceased to bother him. He ruminated that maybe he was totally wrong; the girl was simply an angel, and she surely treated everybody well. It went through his mind that what was happening was that she had a shitty contract and either she had to be nice or she'd be out on the street, without compensation or anything, which was typical of the liberal model of American society. He couldn't decide which of the two options to go with, but he realized he'd like to see her again, invite her out to the cinema and all that. He smiled. He turned his head towards the counter and there she was, enchanting and archangelic, serving a new customer, promptly and efficiently. He thought how foolish he was and how much he needed a coffee.

In Borders there was a standard café where they served a standard coffee (*we call that regular*, they said) on some standard tables. A café where the standard was to sit and read what you'd just bought, as if you were desperate to look at it or had a standard need to show the other aspiring eccentrics that you'd just bought a non-standard book, that you were going to read it, that you wanted to share your solitude but didn't dare, that you'd like that girl or that guy to come over and talk about literature or film, about Borges or Stendhal, Paul Auster and Gore Vidal, about Gus Van Sant's latest film, or Almodóvar's. You'd like that but it never happened. Nothing ever happens when all you have for support are standard inhibitions. Somebody has to make the first move, but Francis wasn't in the mood for moves, backwards or forwards. Francis wasn't in the mood for anybody, for anything, not even for offering up standard conversation starters (*Have you read Walden? Have you ever heard of a Portuguese writer called Saramago? Which do you prefer, poetry or essay, I mean?*), not for this and not for opening up wounds that were difficult to heal. He already had enough wounds, which bled painfully every so often, with the passing of time and the unexpected assault of nostalgic memories. Nostalgia for love and for company, for intimate moments and shared laughter. Nostalgia for peach skins, for tiger's eyes. Nostalgias like cruel, invasive cancers, metastatic and debilitating, steeped in the worst escabeche of himself and the melancholy of other bodies.

For the time being he was quite happy with the material he had bought and with a few references about the author and his work he would be able to look up in some specialist publications in the University of California at Santa Barbara, where he had friends and easy access. He thought about it as he enjoyed the coffee. *Regular*, they said, which meant "so-so" in his native Galician, but it seemed pretty good to him, as if they had confused either the word or the blend, as if it was the last coffee he would ever have, as if there was no coffee as aromatic and full-bodied as this one in the whole world. He began to flick quickly backwards through the copy of *The Stone Raft*. He read two or three lines and then changed page, jumping randomly through a book he knew to be magical. He didn't really know why he had started with that book in particular. Maybe its resemblance to his own ideas about Europe, a place that tried to present itself as monolithic, monochrome, empty of differences and specificities, with its monotonous laws, drowning in a move towards standardization that he considered excessive, forced, doomed to certain failure. Hopeless. He finished his coffee and looked up from his book. He put it down on the table and felt somebody looking at him, intensely and unabashed. It amused him. It was a while since that sort of thing had happened to him. The girl was a blonde, who must have been in her twenties. That amused him even more. He stood up so as not to encourage any more man-eating gazes. There were people who didn't stop to think about what you could get from a look like that, who were terribly anxious to talk but couldn't cross the Rubicon of communication, who argued with themselves behind inscrutable eyes – captive basilisks – and never took the first step in starting a conversation. Like him. Maybe just like him.

On the way to the counter, he wondered whether to have another coffee, switch tables and carry on reading for a while. Those glances made him uncomfortable. He wasn't in the mood for problems or anything like that. He just wanted to get home and rest. These books were enough to be going on with. Maybe soon, in two or three weeks, he would order something else, *The Gospel According to Jesus Christ* or *The History of the Siege of Lisbon*. In a recent interview with a literary journal, the author acknowledged that in the character of Raimundo Silva, a man who falls in love with his publisher, who is much younger than him and saves him from emotional mediocrity, there was something of himself. A good clue. He didn't really understand the concept of emotional mediocrity. Perhaps the author was using a limited concept of feeling. It surprised him. Maybe it was a translation problem. Yes. Most certainly a translation problem. Thinking about it properly, he would order it today. Even though he had no intention of reading it right away. Some books took a long time to arrive. Yes, the one about the man who falls in love with his publisher could certainly be a good way of getting to know the author himself, to guide an exchange of letters and the possible interview. It would be a good opportunity to talk to the African-American shop assistant. Or maybe not. Some other day. When she had nearly forgotten him. When the meeting was a surprise and not an absurd, forced reiteration, on the verge of being suspicious. It would also be helpful to buy some Portuguese music, taking advantage of being in Borders, where they had such a good selection of world music, a term people used to avoid talking about ethnic music, which was seen as old-fashioned, derogatory and politically incorrect. Maybe some fado, some Portuguese folk songs, something that would be a good soundtrack to Saramago's novels.

Having definitively rejected the idea of another coffee, he walked towards the escalator to the music section, which was on the third floor. He looked through the shelves of ethnic music – now the signs revealed the underlying ideology without beating around the bush – a classification as arguable as any other, but good if you're after something exotic, at least from the centripetal point of view of the country you happen to be in. For the Americans, Portugal was as exotic as Timbuktu or Samarkand, Uzbekistan or the Gobi Desert, might be for Francis. A question of where you put the centre of the earth. So very clear for them, the gringo-Americans, and so very inevitable for everybody else.

The fado section was relatively easy to find. There were things by Carlos do Carmo and Amália Rodrigues, cornerstones of Portuguese emigrant nostalgia in the four corners of the earth, their music was all commonplaces and superstores, but they had star quality and filled the boxes at the Olympia in Paris. For other musicians he would have to look in more specialized shops or ask Rui, Professor of Portuguese in Santa Barbara, where there was a Department of Lusophone Literature. He paid by credit card – a rite, a routine, a trap – and headed for the car.

Once on the beach road, he thought of phoning Rose to get together for dinner. Today there was a magnificent sunset and it was silly not to take advantage of it. Anyway he had to talk. He needed to talk. He had a hunger for dialogue, for conversation, for confrontation, for somebody to listen to him. He tapped in the number and immediately remembered they had arranged to meet at eight. He would cook. Grilled fish and a surprise. At eight. Agreed.

On the way home, he stopped at a store with a liquor licence. In the doorway one of the many beggars – every day there were more of them – who wandered the roads of San Rafael was mumbling away. Francis hesitated for an instant. Two dollars more or less didn't mean much for his finances and could give some happiness to that poor beggar. Some happiness and something to eat. He thought that was fair. If he was going to spend fifteen or twenty dollars buying two bottles of wines it didn't seem fair to ignore a man who already had enough to do just trying to survive. The beggar sat there looking at the two dollar bills with some incredulity. He yawned with a mixture of sardonic smile and respect and let Francis pass.

It was a question of getting a good wine to celebrate the beginning of a new literary adventure, he thought. Who on earth could be thinking now about what the oculist had said to him. It was impossible. A different reality. He could see perfectly and they had just offered him a job. He had to celebrate. They could have a good laugh at the oculist, with his blond hair and greasy pink-sausage face. Anyway, who gets it into their head that there are illnesses like that, with their disconcerting origins and non-existent treatments? A mistake. A mistake that wouldn't stand up to another review of his notes by a more confident doctor. All the sausages were stopping up the blood vessels to that yokel's brain. He was one of those arrogant people who start talking without waiting to see if their brain is connected or not. Then whatever happens, they just talk nonsense, without thinking about the consequences. They hear themselves and can't believe their own eloquence, they sound like expensive professionals, brought up amid cotton sheets and plenty of silver. They would have a good laugh at the oculist! He would celebrate his new project. They would celebrate it, he corrected himself. There were two of them, himself and Rose, his sweetheart from the cinema. A lavish dinner and a wine to lift the spirits. A good wine, yes siree, the sort that knock-off quack wouldn't know how to appreciate. A full-bodied red was what Rose liked. He did too, although in less generous measures. They were characteristics. Not everybody could be the same. Those perfect couples, reproducing the breed, top quality, repopulating the world with transgenic children, could be understood only in future Noah's Arks or TV series about shipwreck survivors.

On the shelves were a huge variety of drinks, vodkas and imported champagnes (the "imported" was added, naturally, for the biggest snobs, the ones who followed the trends prefabricated by gurus for yuppies, that emerging category of fauna, for whom quality is in proportion to price and label; in other words, to advertising), whiskies of all kinds, rather more typical of Anglo-Saxon culture, and wine of every origin and type, Australian and Chilean, Bulgarian and Italian, Riojan and French, especially French, which were the favoured indulgence of all the arrivistes (more expensive and not necessarily better) and of course American wines. Then he thought how lucky Americans were. If the Germans had got there instead of the Castilians it would all be sausages and beer instead of that magnificent wine and the ubiquitous Mexican food.

He looked for a Portuguese wine – it seemed an obvious choice in the circumstances – and besides Francis knew about them from recommendations and the odd journey to Portugal, and he knew about their quality and good price, but the store had a very poor selection, limited to the most expensive port and the odd sweet Madeira. He bought two bottles of Los Carneros Reserve, a red from the Napa Valley in California, a jewel of flavours and aromas. A real gift for the senses, with its scent of blackcurrant and American oak, a delicate aroma of ground almond and gooseberry. A luxury for the senses. A luxury Rose deserved. Him too, but especially her. That was why she was the apple of his eye, the sweet love of his life.

When he left the liquor store the beggar didn't recognize him and mumbled his constant request again: *some change, some change*. At first Francis felt rather offended, as if it was some kind of betrayal. Hadn't he already given him two dollars? Didn't he recognize him or was he taking him for a fool? He headed for the car as the beggar muttered reproaches, too weak to raise his voice any louder. Other customers passed him by and he carried on with his mantra: *some change, some change.* People weren't paying him much attention and the man alternated curses with the continual request for change. When he got to the door of the convertible Francis stood looking carefully at the beggar. He thought that maybe he had lost his senses, his short-term memory and his sense of direction, his sensitivity to the cold and perhaps his vision. It occurred to him that he too was going to lose his sight, even now he needed glasses and afterwards even glasses wouldn't do him any good and he would have to wear dark glasses, the glasses of a blind man, handicapped, disabled, a useless man. For an instant he stood looking in turn at the beggar, the sky, the car, the nothingness. He unfocused his eyes and felt the images becoming imprecise, blurred, ethereal like in the half-dream as we pass from waking to sleep, or when we cry and the tears score our eyes, or when we look into a steamed-up mirror, or when we feel sick, feel our legs buckle and fall without knowing how, fainting, broken, uncontrolled, blind.

He got into the car and switched the focus of his obsession. Now it wasn't so much the onset of blindness, which he didn't feel as something real, but rather the arrival in his mind of those depressing ideas. He had to see another doctor, ask for a second opinion, not settle for that fatalistic diagnosis that disturbed him so, coming every few seconds into his mind, repeating itself stubbornly in his head, without him being able to avoid it, incapable of fleeing it, again and again, like a Möbius strip or a curse of Sisyphus. He had to clear his mind of those depressing ideas. He had to fight with resolve and decision to adapt himself to a new situation. He was alive and had strength and the desire to work. He couldn't give in now he had projects and a life before him. He was still too young to give up because somebody, however much of a doctor he was, had diagnosed him with a dramatic condition with no more credibility than a shaman in the equinoctial forest.

Two blocks further on he stopped again. This time to buy tobacco and some matches. He wasn't much of a smoker, just seven or eight cigarettes a day. What he could cadge, or at least what people would stand him. The doctor had told him that smoking was the last thing he should be doing, all tobacco did was accelerate the degenerative process that was beginning in his retina. How stupid! Doctors always say the same thing. It's like a mantra. Don't smoke or drink. It was all the same, whether he went blind in six months or six months and a week. The sentence was there, merciless and terrible, no way back. He paid by credit card and went back to the car. Stop smoking! How stupid!

Francis had a regular fishmonger very close to home, a Chinese immigrant who gave him the best raw ingredients for his cooking. He had met him soon after arriving in San Rafael and since then he hadn't found anybody he could trust more. They greeted each other cordially and with the warmth that comes from habitual contact and mutual respect. For dinner Francis had decided on some fillets of Pacific salmon, smoked and treated with fennel (quite a discovery) for a starter, and some belly fillets of tuna for a really substantial and richly-seasoned main course.

Huo, the fishmonger, smiled approvingly at his choice and they talked a little about how to prepare it. Huo was a skilful kitchen stylist. Few ingredients in each dish, that was his slogan. The important thing was to bring out the natural flavours, he said. Pair each fish with the ideal condiment to bring out its specific flavour. He didn't advise using ginger. "Very strong," he said, "it will mask the flavour of the tuna." Better to use something simpler, like a stuffing of mushrooms and sea-urchin eggs. Francis didn't think a stuffing of sea-urchin eggs and mushrooms was that simple, but he let him talk. In any case Huo would explain the process, he would enjoy the preparation and both he and Rose would enjoy the results, which he suspected would be interesting.

Francis liked Huo, always so judicious in his comments and so attentive. For a moment, while Huo was preparing his order, he thought that if Columbus had got to where he was trying to go, they would have something else in common, and instead of having cousins in Caracas he would have them in Shanghai or in Singapore, and his aunts and uncles from Havana or Artemisa would live in Taiwan, the Island of Formosa, fearful of being invaded by the Chinese giant rather than the American one. He told him that as they said goodbye and Huo seemed to like the idea. Fear of giants. Columbus's journeys. Cousins in Singapore.

When Francis left, Huo wished him good luck with the romantic dinner. It amused him, why deny it? One day he would have to invite him to dinner. Good old Huo, so obliging and so discreet, so mysterious and so different.

5

As Rose parked the car in front of the veranda, Francis placed the tuna bellies in the oven and put the finishing touches to the garnish on the cold plate of salmon, which he seasoned with capers and orange juice (his own recipe, or one he thought of as his own, an experiment carried out successfully at different dinners and with different people – no better or worse, just different). As he uncorked the bottle to let the wine breathe, the outside door opened to reveal a splendid Rose, naturally blonde thanks to her genes and dark from generous exposure to the sun and permanent candidacy for skin cancer. He had warned her many times but Rose wouldn't give in. The UV rays were a constant in her life. Francis was smitten by her, so bronzed and beautiful, so he didn't overdo the negative comments. He came up with the peculiar and somewhat ironic category of telematic-dipsomaniac, but he only thought it and didn't say it out loud, to avoid offending her. Love is not blind, but discreet, he thought. And so, as Rose made her way into the house, his eyes clouded over and he was unable to imagine telling her about his illness; the opportunity to talk about it, the need for a second opinion, the urgency to free himself from the mooring post, all of this brought him to the edge of a continental shelf that disappeared into the abysses of fear, held back by the need to be prudent rather than alarmist.

Rose smiling, insinuating an assault, with her flowered wrap and immaculate teeth, like a commercial for toothpaste or a trendy dentist's surgery, approaching Francis with feline rhythm, sinuous as ivy, the suggestion of ardent kisses, carnivorous sex, sharp nails and unrestrained instincts.

Francis smiling, waiting like an animal poised to pounce, in permanent heat, herbaceous flexibility and anxious kisses, potential energy and muscles tensed by nerves and those almost-forgotten gym sessions.

Francis and Rose. Rose and Francis. Smiling. Kissing. Holding each other close like mushroom tendrils or the scaly rhizomes of quaternary pteridophytes. Experiencing the joy of seeing each other again. Foreseeing futures and pleasures. Hungry for smoked salmon. Tongues preparing the ground, making strategic attacks, with the snaking movements of venomous cobras. Hungry for tuna. With lips that sought and found each other, that transmitted wetness and gentle nibbles. Hungry for everything.

The alarm on the kitchen clock (an ultramodern, lemon-coloured, Sunday-supplement stopwatch, a gift from some enthusiastic friend, a compulsive shopper, gently blackmailing us with supposedly useful presents, to make us introduce order into our lives, time our culinary craftsmanship, delimit territories) ripped through that slow embrace just as the sun set over the immensity of the Pacific, on its way to Japan and the Far East, where everything is born and reborn.

Francis went into the kitchen to turn off the oven and let the belly fillets rest in the warmth. Meanwhile, Rose went for the bottle of red, to help, to begin the ritual of the toast. They toasted the present, as you do when relationships are going well and enjoying a harmonious, steady equilibrium.

They also toasted the future, both immediate and not so immediate, with the hopefulness of those who don't want to fall into the rational temptation of thinking that all stories have an end. Forever. Always and forever, as if they could control the future through will, as if they had some control over their environment, as if they wanted to give shape to their fears by murmuring their desires out loud. As if shooting stars had some kind of power.

"To the future," Rose said, raising her glass.

"To possible futures," Francis answered, touching his glass to hers in a soft clink, which hung in the air, revealing the quality of the glasses.

The ritual over, hands entwined, gazes frozen in viscous air, blinking convulsively from the cold, with the childish gestures and other foolish traits of textbook lovers, they attacked the salmon and the Los-Carneros-Reserve red, a treasure trove of aromas in perfect alchemy.

They put down their glasses as Francis, still standing, served up the dinner with the skill of an adept hotelier or an etiquette manual, rather rigid and a little old-fashioned. Rose hugged Francis from behind. She nuzzled his neck with a slow kiss, lowered her hands to his chest and squeezed it, as if testing the structure of his pecs, measuring the elastic resistance of the muscles. She pressed his nipples, which hardened immediately at the intimate touch. Francis caressed her hands, leaving them to carry on their passionate work that made the down on his arms and the hairs on his chest stand on end. Rose finished with two kisses in the crook of his scalene muscle (which will only seem improper to those with the limited sexual etiquette of the whiner who rarely seeks pleasure, like a hairy and primitive animal, only good for the most violent and brutal procreation) and then she halted her attack and ruffled his hair, like you do to your friends' children.

"I'm hungry," Francis said, removing Rose's hands from around his neck.

"I'm starving too," Rose replied going towards her chair. Sitting down. Smiling lazily and admiringly at her man, her lover, her pluperfect future.

"We'll have plenty of time for other emergencies," added Francis as, with the skill of a craftsman, he rolled up a slice of salmon so the capers wouldn't slip out of the sides.

Rose agreed automatically, lowering her head and concentrating on her starter, focused and unhurried, chewing each morsel carefully, with pleasure.

Once the starter was finished they served themselves more wine, Rose praised the dish again, and Francis automatically murmured his thanks, a compromise, which indicated that he wanted to get up from the table and go to the kitchen for the main course, that he had a hidden pain behind his retinas, that he wanted to and didn't want to, that he was sad and happy, felt comfortable and uncomfortable, didn't know what to do, what to think, what to say.

The belly fillets were competition standard, perfectly cooked and salted (difficult to measure because of the sea-urchin-egg stuffing, which changed the natural balance of salting the tuna). Their celebration of the result led to some intimate caresses, hands stretching out to caress each other from wrist to fingertip, blinking, moistening upper lips with the tips of their tongues, a perfect picture of seduction and lubriciousness, the mythical gesture of the drag queen, provocative in her methods, but innocent in her attempt to change the world order.

After the moment, which seemed taken from a romantic soap opera, a TV series, or a photostory for naive adolescents, Francis rose from his seat to get dessert. Normally they would have a scoop of strawberry ice cream (Rose's favourite) or raspberry (Francis's favourite) or blackberry (a compromise and a discovery), but Francis had spent a peaceful afternoon in the kitchen (perhaps that was why he had gone into the kitchen, to free himself from anxiety or guilt, as so many people do) and he had made a dessert, a lemon-cream tart from a family recipe that would convince the greatest unbeliever, and which provided a magnificent epilogue to a dinner that had promised romance from the start.

"The tart is magnificent. Where did you get it?" Rose asked, amazed by the lemony taste that made her wince, closing her mouth and eyes to bear the acid.

"I made it, idiot. I can't believe you're asking a question like that," Francis replied, half annoyed, half amused.

"I'm sorry, sweetheart. It's so good I can barely believe it. If it was from a cake shop it wouldn't be right with so little sugar. Since it's home-made that's a different matter."

"Alright, madam. In other words if it is good it can't be mine."

"I didn't say that," replied Rose, somewhat confused. "The salmon was very good and the belly fillet was magnificent. I didn't know you were a dessert expert. We always have ice cream for dessert."

"It's easier. It takes a long time to make a tart."

"You're a genius, sweetheart. I didn't mean to wound your pride," said Rose, soothingly.

"Forgiven, darling, but next time I'm buying ice cream from the supermarket, it is less work and you won't pull that disgusted face."

"It's the ice, love. Don't be so sensitive."

"I am."

"I know and I like it. It's one of your charms."

The night was clear, with lots of stars and lots of light. There was a faint breeze and so they decided to sit outside, on the bench by the door. The sea was glittering with silvery reflections of pelagic life, and Francis's eyes were glittering with tears of anxiety and fear as he told Rose first the good and, straight afterwards, the bad news. It was a perverse order, a friendly approach, then the stab of the blade, twisting in the guts.

The news received a varied reception. Rose's face went from a generous, satisfied smile to a rictus of pain and tragedy foreseen. It was a clear night, but they had to open another bottle of wine to put their taste buds to sleep, to be able to cloud their minds and not think of what was to come. A life suddenly and unexpectedly overshadowed. A relationship condemned to the tragedy of mutual support, the lack of independence, the need to adjust to other coordinates and a virtual space, without light and without limits.

There are days when we can sense Atlas's fury at himself and at humanity. On such days the vault of the sky seems to shatter into a thousand pieces and black clouds arrive from who knows where, with little warning and faster than is normal for the season. Just then you hear a thunderclap, and then another, and a smell of ozone floods the atmosphere, while rain upon rain upon rain pours down.

A flash of lightning illuminated Rose's horrified eyes – horrified by the vision of a blind lover, clouded over by the first tears of surprise or rage, paralyzed by the perfect ex-future, frozen by the fear of not knowing what to do, her harmonious order disturbed, lost in a sea of doubts and not knowing how to swim or find a foothold to calm her mind, which is going in all directions and bringing her unwanted images of guide dogs, a blind man's dark glasses, a blind man's faltering walk, a blind man leaning on his cane, a bad-tempered blind man, a father who cannot see his children, a man who saw, who knows about colours and shapes and is going to lose them, of tragedy and the imperfect world, shattered into slicing splinters of ice.

They trailed indoors, barely communicating, silent, not looking at one another.

"Don't be afraid, Rose. I'm not, and I should be shitting myself."

"..."

"Don't be afraid, Rose."

"I'm not," said Rose, as if awaking from a dream, "I know we'll be able to deal with it."

"It's a challenge."

"A great challenge, my love, very great," repeated Rose, like a sententious sibyl or a diviner of letters and sea shells.

The wine brought forth the most secret, incredible hopes – a miraculous cure, a remarkable medicine, a risky and novel operating technique. One glass and another glass gave way to one disappointment and another disappointment, and lies, and lethargy, the desire to sleep rather than make love – not tonight, my mouth is dry, I've got a headache, I'm really tired, maybe tomorrow when we wake up to the sound of the waves. By touch. Trembling evasion. Faces reflecting a new fear. The illumination of the light bulb giving way to silence, incredulity, torpor and a fitful shared sleep full of ceaseless tossing and turning.

In the night they woke up bathed in sweat, embracing like thousand-tentacled anemones, as if an immense fear, intangible but ubiquitous, made them shiver without cold and exasperate each other with interminable nightmares. Francis was uncomfortable, soaking wet and incredibly hot. He threw off the sheets and glanced at Rose, so sensual and so attractive. She murmured unintelligible words, but Francis was already kissing her lips to interrupt her breathing, to make the hair on her shoulders stand up with the soft brush of his nails, to wake her up properly, far beyond half-sleep and nightmares.

Francis was real. Francis wasn't the imaginary character of her fantasies or her dreams. She liked Francis. She liked how he treated her, with that mixture of sweetness and strength, perfectly balanced, with breathless assaults and steady retreats, so as not to tire, not to finish too soon with that typically masculine relief, bloated with urgency. Francis took his time. Francis knew what she liked and did it, again and again, with growing intensity. He caressed her hips with his tongue, relaxed and parsimonious, moved almost indolently down towards the curve of her knees, continued to her ankles and worked his way, slowly and deeply, one by one, across the eight hollows between her toes. They changed position, turned on their transverse axes, rotated, let themselves be caressed on the neck and the shoulder blades, tried out a tectonic movement like the San Andreas Fault, full of fracture and slippage, a tango between slate tiles and stone, honey on hair. They reached a simultaneous climax just at the moment when the storm illuminated the room with textbook lightning bolts, like special effects from a big-budget horror film. Then they sank into a soft state of relaxation.

Francis stretched out his hand towards the night table and took a cigarette from the packet with its camel and pyramids. His favourite tobacco since childhood, when he smoked the chocolate version every Sunday. He lit up and began smoking and thinking about blindness. He smoked and looked at Rose's breasts, so round and perfect, so cared for and formed to the taste of *Cosmopolitan*, so discreet and not excessive, so familiar and so precious. He thought of how little time he had left to see them, how the blindness would advance, inexorable and cold.

As he smoked the storm moved off. It was heading south, towards Santa Barbara, San Luis Obispo and Southern California, the land where they say it never rains.

"I had a terrible nightmare," said Rose.

"Me too," Francis agreed, confused.

"I dreamed about a boy walking along a dirt track. It was a strange track, as if it came out of a desert, bordered by rocks and cactus. The boy was kicking a barrel, like those oak barrels that were used to hold wine."

"They still are," Francis interrupted.

"You're from a strange country. Strange and odd like few others, lost in the mists of time."

Rose continued her story. She made a gesture of acknowledgment, but didn't change the tone of her voice or the structure of the story. She simply carried on talking, as if Francis hadn't said anything, as if Francis wasn't real, as if she were talking to herself, like when she was a child.

"The boy was kicking the barrel and singing the refrain of a song, just the refrain, obsessively and repeatedly. Again and again those words I just can't remember. Suddenly the barrel struck a rock and lost its balance, was flung into the air, as if into the void, then he watched it smash against another rock, and all its contents flew out."

"Wine?" asked Francis.

"No."

"What, then?"

"Scrotums. Hundreds. Thousands of scrotums. It was horrible," said Rose, making a gesture of discomfort and horror.

"And what did the boy in your dream do?"

"I don't know. I woke up right then, when the testicles poured out of the barrel. I didn't see the boy's face, but I think he must have been blind."

"Emasculated and blind. With his eyes torn out after committing incest," exclaimed Francis, irritated, "Like Oedipus revived."

"What? What are you talking about? It's my dream and I didn't dream about any incest. I dreamed about a boy who was carrying a barrel full of scrotums."

"I'm just being silly. Association of ideas. Homespun mythologies. Spurious relationships. Nothing."

"Sometimes you frighten me, sweetheart. It's like you had an undercurrent of madness."

"We all have an undercurrent of madness. If not, life would be unbearable."

"Perhaps, but those things frighten me."

The words hung in the air. There was an unusual flash of lightning, which split the sky. Rose and Francis moved towards each other, uncertain and prisoners of panic.

Rose broke the shell of silence, asking Francis:

"And what did you dream about, sweetheart?"

Francis hesitated, as if it was impossible for him to reply to such a simple question, as if telling it inspired him with fear or respect. Another flash of lightning, this time less powerful, illuminated the sky announcing that the storm was passing; it left them abandoned and tense, orphaned of light. Francis sat up in bed, plumped the pillow behind him, and began:

"I dreamed about blindness. I dreamed I was blind and I was reading Braille, that I spent entire afternoons sitting on a stool beside a window, reading Balzac or Dostoyevsky, Stendhal or Melville."

"When was that?" asked Rose, "It's years since anybody's read Balzac if they're not forced to at school."

"I don't know. It was an unreal time, I suppose, as unreal as the dream itself. What I remember perfectly is that they were all dead authors, as if the action was taking place in the last century, or in a literature department where the only thing that's taught is the work of a bunch of dried-up mummies."

"Mine was more terrifying. You were only reading Braille."

"No. More things happened. Without knowing why I saw myself trapped in a political conspiracy. The enemy's messages were transmitted in Braille and only a blind man could interpret them."

"And what happened?"

"They tortured me. They tortured me into delirium."

"On a rack, like your countrymen in the Inquisition," said Rose rather provocatively.

"Don't start that. I've told you that a lot of that isn't true, and that in Galicia it was always difficult to find executioners prepared to work for the Holy Office, a Castilian thing, people with other preoccupations and other methods. That isn't the point. The point is that in my dream they cut off the tips of my fingers."

"That was all?"

"You don't think that's a lot? It hurt terribly. And what hurt me most is that I would not be able to read any more, deprived of the only form of reading left to me, deprived of feeling in my fingers, useless for delight and pleasure."

"It must have been terrible."

"It was. They went one by one, as if savouring each massacred finger. Flaying it first, then pricking the flesh with pincers. The torturer's face was terrifying. A deformed, cruel man, with a prominent brow and the eyes of a hawk. A being from another world, full of rage and hostility, crazy and sad at the same time. The face of a madman, alienated, like Marlon Brando as Kurtz in *Apocalypse Now*. Remember?"

"Perfectly. The day we met in the cinema."

When he finished his story they decided to try and catch up on the lost hours of sleep. It was warm. So very warm that they fell asleep with the sheets discarded on the floor.

The storm disappeared into the distance, towards Southern California, where it never rains.

6

He felt cold, as if the wind was filtering ceaselessly through the cracks in the wood. He got up. The sea was calm, serene, with that infinite tranquillity that holds back the force of the wind, supports the circadian rhythm of the tides, watches storms pass with a stoic calmness, never moving from its place, returning again and again to caress the beach.

He went to the kitchen for a drink of water. His mouth was dry and his tongue swollen, his head ached as if his temples would burst and a creature was gnawing the inside of his stomach. These were old habits. He hadn't drunk so much since his student days, back in his home country, where they all went out to drink wine in the afternoons, especially him. That was fortunate for his liver, his wallet and his neurones, so hung over now that they demanded a massive dose of water and antacids, multivitamins and an absence of stimuli. Lots of rest and little noise, less light and lots of water. He closed the blinds that gave on to the beach. The day was already peeking through and the sea glimmered full of light. The sea, full of light, that penetrated his still useful eyes. For how long? Six months, the oculist had said, with the cold-blooded Germanic dryness that ran through his veins, with the certainty of somebody who feels himself superior – mimetic lizard – with the arrogance of one who scorns, who humiliates, who condemns.

He thought of a world without light, in permanent shadows, where the stimuli came through touch, through hypertrophied hearing, the smell-sense of the greyhound, the taste-sense of the beefeater, skilled in the discovery of traces of venom. He thought that to be blind from birth was a sentence or a condition, but to go blind was a greater sentence, a boundless tragedy, a punishment from the gods. To know colours, flashes of light, reliefs, shapes. To have a world constructed on the image and likeness of the real world, filtered by the neurones, but reflecting, representing something measurable. To have a reference system, a place in the world, a cartography of your own, and to lose it. To lose your references and measurements, your sense of judgment and your familiar images. Thinking about it, sight was also a permanent illusion. He closed one eye, centred his vision, and the objects changed place. They moved. He did a test. He opened and closed first one eye and then the other. Like that, in a syncopated, puerile, hurried, ridiculous way. An illusion, within an illusion, within an illusion. Our sight deceives us. Things we think are fixed and immobile change with perspective. The image created was just that, an image, and not the reality that vanished in every shift in focus, in every movement of the eyes. He thought that this explanation was one of the most stupid things he had ever come up with, a ridiculous justification, an attempt to conceal the truth. He was going to go blind. Yes, it was possible that the oculist was wrong, but it was more likely he had been right, in a few days it would be the end of one world and the beginning of another, terrible, cruel, different. Scary!, he thought. To lose everything. To lose everything and just be left with the memory. The memory of red and white, blue and yellow, the memory of the greens of the beech trees, the chestnut trees, the wheat in the fields and the lettuces growing even on the plate, the green of the pine trees and the glades of a thousand greens and a thousand shadows. And of course to lose the memory of the blue of the sea and the summer sky, the green of the sea and the spring sky, the grey of the sea and the cloud-laden sky of an autumn of dead leaves, lingering in the humus, of the black, reflectionless sea and the black clouds, full of water and full of winter.

He was convinced that to go blind at forty was an even greater sentence. His other senses were dulled, drowsing in bland apathy, where they barely responded to any stimulus. The din of the city and the din of the house, not to mention other more specific noises, meant his hearing was damaged forever and had very limited registers. What was there to say about smell, barely used in a world where everyday smells had disappeared, for now the streets no longer smelled of freshly-ground coffee, shredded coconut, chocolate factories or bread ovens; everything was equalized by an ignoble levelling where a growing percentage of the population suffered from recurring allergic rhinitis, where there was a unique and omnipresent smell, of burned fuel mixed with food scraps and the clouds of unknowable fumes that came out of the chimneys of power stations or factories, through the grilles of the sewers or the storm drains with their black waters. Taste was dimmed by coffee and tobacco, by the perennial flavour of glutamate and preservatives, vanillin and lemon essence, a flavour unique to ready meals, which always have that sweet taste of cooked corn, which they always try to conceal with excessive doses of pepper – last resort of the junk-food eater – creating one solitary sensation on the palate, a mixture of sweet and spicy, hard to define, killing off the multi-toned sensitivity of the taste buds. There was still touch. Touch, yes, the most nostalgic of the senses. But who to touch? Who to touch without causing offence? What to feel if he had never felt anything without the help of his eyes?

The sea filled up with light, and his eyes rejoiced in the light that was life, joy, the fuel that powered his biological triggers, that was all he knew and might lose, that was the essence of a life, the refrain of a song.

The hangover was always the same, a descent into hell in order to realize that heaven exists, is there, in balance and moderation, in this life and not in another, possible or dreamed. He thought that was foolishness, it wasn't a case of thinking it over and over, there was no need to wallow in a sea of guilt, in permanent self-criticism, the negation of any enjoyment, the misery of your own abyss. They were the defects of a baseless education, heaps of memorizing and little reasoning, plenty of dogma and few explanations, all certainties and no doubts. Francis liked doubts. Having them and getting over them, losing them and re-encountering them. Concealing them in your most intimate places or scattering them to the four corners of the earth, depending on the case, the company, and your spirit. Certainties scared him. Always had. Ever since childhood. Like darkness and silence. Like torture and fire.

He got back into the bed, which was warm and welcoming. Fortunately, Rose still hadn't woken up. Fortunately, he thought, because Rose tended to react wildly in the morning, grabbing his pillow or shouting idiocies at him, howling like a wild beast or biting him on the lips. Rose was rather excessive in everything, physically and temperamentally, the way she smiled and the way she woke up, her words like slabs of stone and her flights into the future, never looking back, not believing in crossroads. A special woman, of heroic stock, the sort you could count on the fingers of one hand. He had been lucky to find her. Lucky too that she had fallen for somebody like him who could pass for her older brother (body of a veteran athlete, where the tricks of age were calling him to account in wrinkles and joints, in diverse decrepitudes and an absence of flexibility, in games consumed by time and many limitations). Within moments, he was asleep.

When he awoke again, he sought Rose out between the sheets. She wasn't there.

The light bothered him and his eyes itched. He had an octopus scratching at the inside of his left eye, sucking at him with its suckers and bothering him with its parrot-like beak that tapped at his temples. A metallic taste, like the zinc of an old bathtub, rose up from his stomach, burning his chest. A terrible nightmare tortured his lower stomach and wouldn't go away.

He went to the bathroom to see if he could begin the ceremony of reconstructing the harmonious equilibrium of his body. From there he called to Rose. Nobody replied. Then he realized he was alone, Rose had left him alone. Without saying goodbye. The only sign of life was Lucretius, the two-coloured kitten, at the swinging door where he came and went from the house with total freedom (one might call it impunity).

Lucretius had been a gift from Rose, "so you won't be so alone in the beach house," she had said, as she opened an immense cage and let Lucretius loose into the living room, to scratch the sofa out of pure confusion, to bite on the cushions of the winged armchair, to cover the carpets with the fur of a fearful and just-pissed cat. Francis had never liked household pets, which he considered an extra burden on top of all the existing household tasks. A burden and one more tie. That's what he had thought before the arrival of Lucretius, who now kept him company from a distance, with his mere presence, his air of independence as he crossed the room or appeared at the bathroom door, scaled the back of the sofa or disappeared into the garden to enjoy the sun or carry out an expedition in search of other members of his species. He had to admit Rose had been right, for she had made him lose one of his prejudices (another one), had given him an omnipresent but discreet companion, whom he could play with and also talk to about serious things, with whom he could have long rambling conversations like on a psychoanalyst's couch or enjoy a spontaneous and growing complicity.

They had called him Lucretius by pure coincidence, because when Rose came in bearing the gift – over the top as ever in her dress and her language, a powerful woman – she asked Francis, "How are you today, darling?" and he, lifting his head up from his book, replied, "Here, with Lucretius," and so the little creature became Lucretius, with his two colours and lively air, a Lucretius reborn in an unexpected and difficult reincarnation.

Everybody has their own hangover cure. There were no miracles or magical remedies. Francis's body, outraged by alcoholic excesses, needed to recover its fluid balance, and that took time. Everybody has their own method, but the only thing that worked for Francis was not to drink. After a glass of tomato juice (he had read about it in one of those magazines you leaf through on aeroplanes out of interest or disinterest, depending on your state of mind that day), he decided on a leisurely breakfast, as if he were a bird feeding on grain. He had quit his hurried, pre-shave orange-juice habit, and his post-shower coffee followed by the day's first cigarette, in favour of seeing breakfast as the most important meal of the day. A fruit shake, with mangoes and oranges, bananas and apples, two slices of cheese on toast, some porridge with a teaspoon of olive oil, a coffee with biscuits and a cigarette – ritual addictions that shaped his life – as he browsed the day's agenda.

Today he was entirely free of commitments. Go shopping for the bare essentials, a few calls to friends or colleagues, about upcoming appointments or greetings and congratulations, and little more. The day's focus was the translation job, no professional appointments or choice-free, obligatory lunches. Just systematic research on the author he would have to translate so quickly.

He would have to start reading the books he had bought. He wouldn't start with the novel he was going to translate. It was a technique of his, no better or worse than any other, just the one that seemed easiest to him. Accustom yourself first to the author's world and style by exploring the difficulty of his vocabulary or syntax, his alliterations and digressions, the temporal shifts or paraphrases, so as to be able to calculate the best strategy for the translation and set out the deadlines. He would start with *The Stone Raft*, which he had so often been recommended in the past and had always resisted reading, lost in other priorities or victim, perhaps, of another of the prejudices that fettered his spirit, which he was aware of and tried to overcome, but which were as securely attached as the lichen on the rocks at the shore.

It was almost eleven in the morning. Better to go as soon as possible to Huo's fishmongers and find some fresh fish for the lunch he assumed he would be eating alone. Perhaps with Lucretius, if he wasn't out on the razzle seducing the female kittens in neighbouring gardens, but without Rose, certainly without Rose, who had chores and commitments. Rose couldn't come every day. She got up very early and worked into the night. She had been working for almost three months on a project to expand the computer capacity of a business in San Carlos. It ate up her time, but it was a unique opportunity to make a name for herself at the consultancy where she worked, and, above all, to go from a temporary to a permanent contract. It was an opportunity and she couldn't pass it up. Here there were jobs for everybody, but the good jobs were very rare and the dominant ideology (if not the only one) was based on a professional career, merits, and continued challenges, on going further and further and further until you got to the top. Maybe this was what people thought of as the American Dream, but it didn't interest Francis in the slightest. It might have been a hoary old phrase, but he still preferred working to live rather than the other way round. With Rose it was hard. She had taken the American value system very much into her head, engraved on her frontal lobe, as if when she was little somebody had fired an ideological dart at her and it was still in her, contaminated and forever condemned. With Rose it was hard. Every day a battle. Every week a negotiation to defend their time together, to exchange work priorities for life priorities, to eat some grilled fish rather than a takeaway pizza, which arrived cold and rubbery, as if it were made of plastic and dyed with tomato.

Rose visited him, normally, twice a week and they almost always spent the weekend together at the beach house. For a southern European, brought up in a traditional Catholic Galician family, with a strict Catholic lifestyle, that situation seemed abnormal, anomalous, a constant source of remorse and blame. But the world was changing at a speed that would have given his grandmothers vertigo and his mother a discreet nausea, but which only gave Francis the odd attack of passing perplexity and automatic resignation. The normal thing for professional American couples was to have very independent lives, to be together as much as possible but only when professional obligations allowed. Always prioritizing work, your career, all the accessories. That attitude had also travelled to Europe and especially to the Anglo-Saxon world, where they adapted so easily to ideas imported from the United States (and vice versa).

They called it the beach house out of habit, to differentiate it from Rose's apartment, which was in the city, where they only rarely met up. Today wasn't a visit day, so he would have to have lunch and dinner alone. Lunch wasn't a problem. He would have a smoothie or a sandwich of some sort, but for dinner he needed something more elaborate. He would go into the kitchen to forget about everything, enjoy himself, have a glass of wine after pounding a sauce in the mortar, at ease and relaxed, a bit tipsy and very happy. Then he would eat at the living-room table in front of the television, like a normal American, like so many average Americans, tall and short, film directors or car mechanics, factory workers or elected senators, all eating in front of the television, watching the basketball or baseball games, making love, masturbating in front of the television, committing suicide or giving birth in front of the television, omnipresent object, anonymous companion, witness of all their crimes.

He went down to the garage and got into the metallic blue convertible. Typical of America. To go and buy fish at Huo's store he had to take the car. And to go to the supermarket, the barber's shop, the bank... you had to take the car for everything. He liked to walk, but there it was almost impossible or even dangerous, because of the distance and because of the strangeness of the very act of walking along the roadside. There was suspicion if you came across the police. Where are you going?

Where have you come from? Where did you leave your car? Papers? Come with us to the station and that whole senseless story they love so much, that band of brutes who take advantage of the pistols and the uniforms to take the lid off their complexes, to abuse those they would have no other way of abusing.

Huo smiled as soon as he saw him come in. He was serving two Mexican women who wanted to buy mahi-mahi. They were arguing about how fresh it was and how to prepare it. They spoke loudly but melodiously, and Huo didn't seem in a rush to get rid of them. Maybe he liked them, thought Francis, one or both of them, as he glanced over the day's specials.

As soon as he'd finished dealing with the Mexican women Huo gave him a friendly greeting and some slices of abalone, or ormer, to try, brought from San Diego Bay, which were much celebrated in California's Japanese restaurants. The sea ear, marinated in a sauce of spicy radish and soy sauce, was delicious and there was a joint celebration, of the discovery and of their shared taste. They agreed – Huo always seemed to reach an agreement, albeit a tacitly-imposed agreement – that Francis would take two ray wings. Huo assured him they were very fresh, just out of the sea, the waters of San Rafael itself, and to prove it he showed him the red drops of still-fresh blood and the texture of the skin on the belly side of the ray, two sure signs, according to Huo, of the fish's freshness. It didn't have eyes or gills to refer to and the buyer had to look for other guiding signs. Huo was an expert and Francis knew it. Huo wouldn't deceive him about the quality of the fish for anything in the world. Loyalty was a characteristic shared by good Galicians and Chinese, despite their differences in tradition and culture.

Huo always made the right choice, his criteria were freshness and the best preparation. This time his advice was more a trick of preparation than an elaborate recipe. He advised Francis to scald the ray in a pot with plenty of boiling water, to which he should add salt and a glass of vinegar, and before it evaporated, to drop the ray wings in for barely a minute. Francis thanked him for the advice, which was a variation on the way his grandmother had shown him to prepare shark and dogfish, common fishes in the family diet, and which he now dredged up from the bottom drawer of memory. Just for comparison. To certify once again the similarities between peoples. To be amazed.

When he got home, Lucretius was stretched out in the middle of the room, a genie or a prince from the *One Thousand and One Nights* in a mansion that had acquired, with his presence, a touch of the orient and Asiatic luxury, of a place for pleasure and meditation, for love and languor, a hidden fragment of paradise from which to watch the passing of time. He went automatically to the telephone and, out of habit or a brief Pavlovian impulse, lit a cigarette. There was a message from Rose, banal and with a hint of duty, remorse, doing what she thought she ought to do after a night of confidences and thunder, love and thunder, thunder and fear. He imagined her during a break from work, between one management meeting and another, having a coffee and smoking a cigarette in the corner reserved for smokers, for the pestilent, for the poor bastards addicted to tobacco, that filthy vice. She would take the opportunity to call him, to leave him a brief message, I'm here and thinking of you, sweetheart, and to say again and again between puffs that she had to give up smoking, her bosses kept an eye on people with habits and she wanted to move on up, rise up like scum, get to the top. There was also a message from Martin, the publisher, to tell him the contracts were ready on his desk, and would he rather have them sent to the house by courier, or come by one day soon to sign them in the office? Either would do, but please call as soon as possible.

Watching Lucretius stretch out, all urgency seemed excessive. In reality Martin was calling to see how everything was going. Francis's state of mind and the progress he'd made with the translation. It was an omen. He had to understand that it was very early to be talking of progress, that just today he had started reading a novel by Saramago and no progress was possible just yet. Martin was good at rushing, physically and mentally, and he was a bad liar. Above all, he was a bad liar. As soon as he heard the message, Francis knew it was just waffle, an excuse thought up when Martin realized there was nobody at home or nobody was going to pick up the phone, which came down to the same thing. From there to thinking that Francis wasn't, after all, working on the translation wasn't a huge step, a very slippery slope where doubts began to appear easily. He would have to call him and calm him down. Tell him that now he had a bibliography, and music, and projects, and that he would start the translation right away, please don't worry, everything's going smoothly. He would get excited and talk about possible delays, illusory deadlines, inexistent commitments and invented emergencies. Martin was like that, hewn from that cloth, and there was no loving him or not loving him, you just had to put up with him and bear him as best you could, lying and hiding out, letting things go and giving no importance to the emergencies of an overexcited executive with fire in his belly.

He thought about it more. He wouldn't call him. He would let him sweat for a couple of days, he could calm down on his own. He wasn't in the mood to be watched, to have Martin following the work day by day as if he was a novice translator who had to be guided from the start so he didn't invent another, different novel, so he was careful with the style, so he didn't produce a version that was too literal or excessively his own and far from the spirit and intentions of the author. They would have a meeting to go over the work, but it was very early – ridiculously early – to give in to the blackmail of daily tormenting control.

He thought of calling Rui, a childhood friend from Porto when they used to go to GNR or Xutos & Pontapés concerts, when they watched the dawn in Boavista or on the beaches at Castelo, on the way to Matosinhos. Rui was a professor in the Department of Romance Languages at the University of California at Santa Barbara. He thought of calling him to talk about the translation he had in hand and to ask about some details of the author's style and syntax. Rui was a friendly guy, very systematic and difficult to pin down, always at conferences or symposiums, giving lectures or travelling for the pleasure of travelling, to India or Mozambique, to Macau or Timor, in search of who knows what, like a character from Tabucchi or Le Clézio, roots or mythologies, it all came down to the same bittersweet sauce of nostalgia.

He thought of calling Rui and he called him. An impersonal and rather adenoidal voice, suggesting a mutilated septum or forced immigration, confirmed his suspicions: Professor Andrade was away travelling. After some investigation – his interlocutor had become friendlier on detecting his Latin accent and had put the call through to somebody in the Department of Romance Languages – he found out that Rui Andrade had left for Cape Verde to study the islands' Creole, which he was trying to connect with the Creole of Macau and the unusual Portuguese spoken in Bahia, which is supposed to be connected with the Galician language. He wondered how to end the conversation with Rui Andrade's colleague, a talkative and very enthusiastic man, rather prolix and not at all pragmatic. He thanked him for the information and hung up before the other man could resume his chat about the importance of Creole and Papiamento, of Melanesian pidgin and other synthetic languages.

He would wait for Rui to get back. Thinking about it, he would be busy for three or four weeks reading the Saramago novels he had bought in Borders, and having a first look at *Ensaio sobre a Cegueira*, which he now held in his hands as a valuable object, with reverence and affection. After this first incursion he would revisit it a couple of times to put together the first draft based on the recording of his oral translation.

It was his method. There were others, but he preferred to start with a spoken version that somebody could put down on paper. After that first draft he could work more quickly. Despite his frequent use of the PC Francis was still quicker with words than keys, and he had used this method for a few years, with results he considered optimal.

The first incursion into *Ensaio sobre a Cegueira* turned out to be something of a struggle. The novel was readable and gripped him from the start. It was, all in all, astonishing, immediately connecting stylistically with a millenarian parable of the destructuring of society and the absence of hope. It didn't leave you indifferent, but getting through it, page by page, became more and more difficult, perhaps because of the absence of physical descriptions of the characters that is so common in the majority of writers. It was going to be a big job, he thought, as he lay back on the sofa to mull over the novel that he foresaw would be his last – perhaps, if medicine found no cure, the very last work he would ever translate. This was a recurring thought that floated up every so often as if recovered from a sea of doubts. Francis tried to dismiss it, but it always returned.

He let these and other thoughts grow inside him, submerging him in anguished unease. He was of the opinion that when a person felt uncomfortable with the job they were doing, the best thing to do was take a break. Lucretius wandered over affectionately and provided him with the first moments of leisure since he had started reading the novel. He played with him and felt that there were still marvellous things in the world that enabled him to grip on to life.

After four or five hours of reading, interspersed with various games with Lucretius, he went to the kitchen.

He always did this when he was at home and depressed, like that Banana Yoshimoto character who said the best place to sleep was next to the fridge, or that the only room where he had always been happy was the kitchen. The thoughts of people from the East, so different from us in their traditions and the structure of their thought, so close to us in their feelings and pleasure in life.

It was still early to get stuck into the task of preparing dinner, so he decided the best thing would be to treat himself to a mixer. He opted for a vodka Martini, which he'd grown accustomed to on his flights with American Airlines, his favourite company, which he always flew with when he could and when his professional or romantic commitments took him away from San Francisco to New York or Chicago. The vodka Martini was explosive, a full frontal attack on the deepest hidden neurones of his brain, so he had to drink it carefully and slowly, and never let the emotion of the first drop lead him to consume it with too much enthusiasm. He put on a CD of Elba Ramalho, a great singer of Brazilian popular music. *Flora*, *Alegria Real* and *Caminhos Do Coração* came on, which began to make him feel rather lukewarm. His homesickness was gaining ground very rapidly when the singer attacked with *Miragem Do Porto* and *Na Hora "H"*. He was already trapped by Elba's enchantment and by the sadness that twined like ivy around his heart. For the first time in a long while he was talking to himself, aloud, like when he was a child, in a more moderated, low voice than the one he tended to have when he heard himself on a recording or a voicemail message, as if articulating more clearly, one sound after another, as if he wanted to hear each sound of his voice, each intonation, each change of tone, each inflection to emphasize a question, to show admiration, to argue a negative or admit a doubt. Another doubt and so few certainties.

He got up from the sofa, looking out at the sea. His lips were barely two centimetres from the window pane, as if he wanted to eat the landscape, as if he wanted to tell the sea everything that was happening to him, causing him anguish, imprisoning his soul. His voice echoed against the living-room windows, creating a strange atmosphere, without music now, of confinement or a torture chamber, a lunatic asylum or death row. The death of light. Madness from the absence of light. The torture of not being able to see. Without music now, he thought aloud. Light is like the music of life, sight like symphony and rhythm. Simple metaphors. Without light now. Blind. Gazing at the sea and dreaming of no longer seeing it. Closing his eyes and trying to trap the sea in his memory. Transported. Hanging from a cord or waving his arms in free fall. Wanting to drink and wanting to be happy. Dreaming that it was all a dream. Taking another sip of vodka Martini.

He went over to the hi-fi and pressed a button to repeat the same CD. He sat down on the sofa. He pushed Lucretius away, and Lucretius realized straight away that his friend wasn't in a good mood and went to his basket without a murmur. Francis finished the vodka Martini and wondered whether to pour himself another or take a walk on the beach. Thinking, with the good taste of a child sure of his own impulses, that the first option would lead him to wallow in the worst of himself, he decided to put down the drink and the self-mythologizing as a defeated hero and go out for a walk on the beach.

He liked to drink, but he also knew his limits. One mixer was good, it relaxed him and made him look at the situation from another perspective. Two could be negative, make him lose control and say or do things that he neither thought nor really wanted to do. He opened the door and took the path to the beach. It was a magnificent day, with a radiant sun and waves perfect for surfing.

When he closed the door, Elba Ramalho's peachy voice was murmuring the last lines of *Eu Vou Te Amar*. Only Lucretius, in the welcoming solitude of his corner, savoured the apotheotic climax of the song. A pity for Francis. A joy, certainly, for Lucretius.

7

There weren't many people on the beach. Four or five lads who preferred their surfboards and contact with the waves to their Maths or English classes, two couples walking their shared solitude along the shore and a Chinese boy, very enthusiastic and rather ungainly, who was trying to fly a kite.

Francis followed the line of palm trees leading to the expanse of sand that sloped down to the coast. He kicked off his trainers and, carrying them, walked down to the shore. He crossed a band of shells and pebbles licked by the waves, felt their touch on the soles of his feet. He closed his eyes tightly and tried to feel his feet, only his feet, only with his feet. To feel consciously, to detect edges and textures, dampness and reliefs. He surprised himself with the variety of stimuli, sensations, registers of touch he hadn't ever stopped to explore. He smiled. This world held many worlds, many experiences, which we almost always pass over unseen, caught up in a needless, textbook rush or strict routine. He sat down, relaxed and somewhat sad from the obsessive focus on his own thoughts. He picked up an abalone shell, with its spiral design whose radius doubles every two quadrants, opening itself up to the outside, allometrically growing to create an unforgettable image, with its little holes on the upper side, its pearly interior, the coloured stripes on its outside. He closed his eyes, let the tips of his fingers slide inside the shell until he felt the smooth mother-of-pearl, feeling around the sides until he could determine the exact shape, until he was able to imagine how the shell could be – in the now impossible future of a dead animal– if it were alive and continued to grow. Then he started to examine the outside, running his fingers over the wrinkles and reliefs, tiny tracks left by different growth spurts. Then he located the little holes parallel to the upper edge. He counted them. Seven. A magic number. Eyes still closed, he blew on the shell and was able to pick out a chorus of fully-nuanced sounds that seemed like something from a fantasy.

He put the abalone shell down and, with his fingertips, explored the surface of the sand around where he was sitting. He touched stones, shells, the remains of seaweed or bits of wood, until, by chance, he came across a conch shell. He repeated all the exploratory movements he had made with the abalone shell and then, his eyes still shut, put it to his ear to listen to the sound that is said to invoke the marine essence of waves and storms, calm periods, and mermaids, crouched in the labyrinthine chambers of the shell. After a while he relaxed his fingertips, feeling as if his mind was opening up to a new world of whitish light and, slowly, he prepared to open his eyes. Looking intensely at the sea, he beat a track to the waves, where he began to play like a solitary child.

There was something of an undertow and his feet became half buried in the sand each time a wave decided to retreat from the beach and return to the sea. He carried on walking, still holding his trainers, thinking about his illness and his future. The waves dragged up all sorts of seashells, clams and abalones with their unique shell in its perfect Archimedean spiral, the little holes lined up along the outside edge, mussels encrusted with serpulid worms and acorn barnacles, shells with inverse rotation, horse mussels, crab shells – empty after being moulted – algae ripped from the seabed by the force of the waves, limpets that came from the cliffs to the north, sands transported a thousand and one times, the remains of fishing tackle, musky-skinned fruits, stones licked by the salty fluid – their edges smoothed, caressed again and again until losing their rock-like appearance, more like gemstones or Neptunian cameos – mermaid's purses, stingrays and wild skate with their twisted horns, squid bones scattered on the sands like the remains of a shipwreck, jellyfish rotting in the sun, asymmetrical sea urchins robbed of a surface to attach themselves to, marine remnants of the most diverse species, cadavers, relics, remains. Everything that landed on the beach was dead, dead after once having known the light, having known life and liberty. He thought about cycles and tides, about how fish let themselves be guided by the stars or hid away in winter, about the stones in their heads that indicated their age, and how people paid extraordinary sums for them. He remembered Pliny. Good old Pliny.

He mused as he left his own trail on the beach. He turned and looked at his tracks in the sand. He looked at them as if it were his last look back at the past, at his trail in the sand and in life, at the road that was now becoming constricted and conflicted, to end in a black tunnel, in a funnel stretching out towards an imperceptible bottom, where one entered only to die, to cease to be, to lose everything. Even dreams.

Perhaps all those musings, all those worries and those thoughts – spurious through their familiarity, their sense of cliché, like a film with a moralizing denouement – were simply a suggestion of the impact the doctors' announcement had had on him. No, not all the doctors. That one particular doctor, that ice-man who had diagnosed that his days were numbered. He still had days of light, of clarity, of seeing Rose's beautiful face, holding out her hand for him to take, moving in to kiss him without blushing, putting her arms around his waist to embrace him, to reassure him, to pull him closer.

His eyes were wet with enormous tears, like the tears of tortoises or crocodiles in children's stories, impossible to contain. If it was something else, a tumour or even AIDS, that fin-de-siècle kick in the butt, it would be different. He was better prepared for death, for its inevitability and its ubiquitous presence, than for a slow and partial demise, being left without a limb or one of his senses. That was worse, far worse. It meant having an incomplete existence, like an absurd mannequin, his abilities stifled, lost in a world that was no longer his own, no longer the one in which he had grown used to living. He would have to learn Braille, something that had always seemed as distant to him as musical notation or Morse code, and as inaccessible, almost, as the Chinese or Cyrillic alphabets, which he had tried to learn in the past with paltry results that did not reflect the suffering they inflicted. It was a question of education and circumstance. His education meant his whole world was built on a system of visual symbols that would now vanish, no longer have meaning, no longer be useful. He was forty now, and it had cost him so much effort to learn the codes of Western civilization, so many years of study and dedication to reading and word games, now it would all come down to the last words, the last tracks in the sand, the last sunsets and the last people walking on the beach.

He bent down and picked up a long, flat stone. He looked towards the sea and threw it so it bounced on the surface of the waves. He immersed himself in the game like he did when he was a child, when he played with his brother to see who could throw furthest or who was able to get the most bounces before the stone was submerged by a wave. As he continued to try, he let his mind go blank, enjoyed it, was happy playing with the stones and the waves, like he did when he was a child, with no great worries, like when he was a child, waiting for somebody to call him in for dinner, like when he was a child, feeling immortal, a super-powered super-hero.

He spent an indefinite period of time in the game and then decided to continue his walk, the water splashing around his ankles. He walked along the shore, savouring the water that rose up in a fine spray or in countless drops, in a curtain of water or watery rags. That was when he lifted his head and saw the Chinese boy who was trying to fly a kite. He looked at the Chinese boy's kite and felt sorry for him. The poor boy didn't even know the first thing about making his magical toy fly. He approached him and in a Latin-inflected English asked if he needed any help. The boy reacted with a certain arrogance, but after Francis feigned disinterest and looked as if he was about to carry on walking, the boy asked him, humbly and with an enormous smile, if he could give him some advice. Francis showed him how to tighten the cord, how to guide the kite towards the wind and how to keep it flying for as long as he wanted by loosening and tensing the string, patiently and attentively. As they were engrossed in these manoeuvres, the Chinese boy's father came over to his son, to make sure the stranger wasn't pestering him. The lad, all naturalness, said:

"This man showed me how to tighten the string."

"OK," said his father with a dutiful smile, "but now we have to go home. Your mother will be worried."

"Take care," said Francis as he turned on his heels to continue his stroll.

The boy was grateful to him, running over to his father and waving goodbye to Francis with a hand that might have been an apprentice in kite-flying, but was an expert in farewells. As Francis continued his walk alongside the waves the boy experimented with the technical knowledge he had just acquired, sharing it with his father, who was happily pulling the string and making the kite fly. Francis said goodbye from a distance and noticed that the boy was still looking at him, grateful and happy, watching as his father demonstrated an unsuspected skill with the kite.

Francis continued his walk, musing on his immediate and not-so-immediate future. The vodka Martini that was circulating in his veins helped to expand his imagination so he could think with a certain objectivity. Once he was further away, he turned around again to see where he had left the Chinese boy and his real father and saw with the pride of a father-who-wasn't, a potential father, that the boy had quickly developed a certain degree of skill in handling the strings and their relationship with the wind. He thought how if he was blind he wouldn't be able to pass on that knowledge to any child, even his own, the ones he wanted but didn't have, not to mention other people's. He pondered the feeling of being useful to others and thought about what he would be able to pass on when those eyes of his, so beloved and so useful, were no longer able to make out shapes, the colours of flowers, the precious half-light of the sun setting on the Pacific. He was thinking about all of this as he passed a blonde woman walking her dog on the beach, with her headphones, and a pair of shorts that revealed some fantastic thighs, sculpted by a thousand and one gym and aerobics sessions.

He thought about the futility of this society and the even greater futility of the European society he came from, where he had been born and grown up, now so dehumanized and so desperate to imitate the Americans, as if the key to the future was no more than a poor adaptation of the American way, that consumerist quagmire that enveloped everything. He passed a rather tired and silent gay couple who looked carnivorously at him, the look of potential predators, the sort of people who would taste any wine, young or not so young. It was a prejudice – another one,

Jeez, they were growing like mushrooms after a day of rain – and he had to cast it out of his mind, but he felt that if he was blind they wouldn't have given him a look like that, even if he managed to keep his body in its current athletic condition. It was a prejudice, he thought, as he turned around to go back home. The surfers were packing up and the sun was crouching, radiant, on the horizon. Tomorrow would be another sunny day. He thought of that and was comforted a little, as he was whenever he ate octopus Illa-de-Arousa-style, sardine empanadas or noodles with clams, his favourite dishes.

Back at home, he went to the kitchen to make dinner. Under Lucretius's watchful gaze, he carefully cleaned the remaining skin on the ray wings; the cat doubtless wanted to share in the feast provided by Huo the fishmonger. As they had agreed, Francis gave him the leftovers from the fish. At first, Lucretius demonstrated a haughty lack of interest, but then he reined in his pedigree pride and set about the aperitif offered by Francis. Francis filled a pie tin with water and a little vinegar. He waited for it to boil and scalded the ray wings, following his experienced fishmonger's advice step by step. He fancied trying something new and decided to prepare the ray with a purée of mild garlic and parsley.

It was one of his maternal great-grandmother's recipes, a stern woman from the Muros area, an expert in fish and childbirth, who had been something of a tyrant, but a great cook too. He began by preparing the garlic purée. He scalded the garlic, peeled the cloves, boiled the chopped-up, hulled pieces for five minutes and tipped them into a saucepan with melted butter and cooked onion. When it all stopped foaming, he added cream and let the mixture reduce by half, stirring continuously. Next he chopped a big bunch of parsley for a salad, and added some sliced almonds, dressing it with oil, vinegar, salt and pepper. After fiddling with the garnish, he put the ray wings in another pan to fry with a sauce of lard, capers and a little parsley. It was already starting to take shape. The smell was flooding Francis's kitchen, Francis's nose, Francis's olfactory bulb, Francis's entire being, all longing to see the finished dish. Once the ray was fried off, he put it in a low oven and let it cook slowly. To kill time while the oven and the patient flame were bringing out the flavours he lit a cigarette and relaxed, gazing out to sea.

The result was epic. Francis had a bottle of young red wine nice and chilled in the fridge, so it was all very easy. He moved the table outside, facing the sea, and let himself be carried away by the aroma and the flavour of the ray wings that brought back so many memories. The setting sun was level with his plate, the cumulus clouds forming a halo around the distant horizon, the dolphins swimming in the twilight, with the lights of San Francisco appearing here and there, their reflections filling the night that was falling now, flooding through everything.

After dinner he settled back into his first, stunned reading of *Ensaio sobre a Cegueira*. It was curious, but despite the absence of physical descriptions he found himself clearly envisaging each of the characters, especially the doctor's wife. It was a task that this particular author left up to the reader. Each reader had to create the physical appearance of the characters, as deeply-felt presences, as the material form of the characters that the author had made such an effort to sketch out. It was a step forward. Francis had always had this defect. He was unable to proceed with a story unless he could imagine the physical appearance, especially the faces, of the different characters who inhabited a story. Sometimes the author made it very easy, sketching out the features of this or that face, a Roman nose, wide-set eyes, the curl of the eyelashes, an eavesdropper's ears, cheeks pocked by fever or acne. This was different, you had to work constantly to give a face to the faceless, to advance along the shingle path of action. It was a first reading, and the difficulty of the first few pages (absence of orthographic markers, a re-encounter with Portuguese, a language so close to his geographical universe, a beloved language that felt very close to him) gave way to a much more rapid reading. The novel picked up speed and carried Francis along with it, helpless before the author's unquestionable skill.

It was around eleven when Rose called to find out about his day and how he was feeling.

"How are you?"

"Fine. I'm having dinner, ray wings and a glass of wine."

Then she asked if he had noticed anything wrong with his sight or if he needed anything. It wasn't a good time for Rose to call; she seemed agitated, unsure, nervous. Nobody called after ten if it wasn't something serious. Rose usually didn't, either. Francis talked enthusiastically about the novel, avoiding the low spirits he had had after the vodka Martini, when he had gone to walk off his melancholy on the south beach at San Rafael. Then he told her about what he had eaten and how good it would be if she were there, how much he loved her, wanted her, needed her all the time. The talk of unrestrained lovers, fearful of solitude and panicked by silence.

"No. I won't drink too much. I have to work."

"…"

"It's OK. Don't worry. I'll expect you tomorrow. What do you want to eat? Don't tell me you don't want fish. You've got plenty of time to eat those hamburgers you like so much when I'm not around."

They said goodbye until the following day, when Rose would try to find a gap in her work diary to come and have dinner with Francis. Rose's career was very important to her, she had got herself a very good contract, and in such a competitive society, where there were a hundred sharks waiting for her to lose it, she couldn't allow herself any frivolity. It was quite frivolous enough to be going out with a Spaniard (he insisted he was Galician, but the Americans didn't go in for details and for them he was a Hispanic, like those tortilla-eating Mexicans or the Cubans who couldn't live without their pork and beans) who was a fish-eater and the English translator of an almost-unknown Portuguese writer. Who the hell was that writer who couldn't write in English like Auster or DeLillo, Robbins or Anne Rice? What was the point of writing in a language other than English if all the computer programs were in English, if business was done in English, if ninety-five out of the world's hundred best writers wrote in English? A bohemian. Rose was going out with a bohemian. That might well have been very chic in Europe where the generation of free love and environmentalism still reigned, but there, in America, there was no point in going out with a loser, with somebody who wasn't involved in finance or information technology. If he had even been a lawyer there would have been some hope, but a Portuguese-English translator and a Hispanic who didn't want to be called a Hispanic, on top of everything, was just too much.

Francis stayed up for another couple of hours. The local TV channel was showing the baseball game between the San Diego Padres and the Dolphins, from Florida. Francis had been a fan of the Padres ever since he had arrived in California. They were the most real team, the closest to the normal people, the Latinos and Taiwanese, the Vietnamese and Italian immigrants. They all shouted, "Go Padres!" each of them with their own accent, Saxon or Sicilian, Asian, Mexican or Portuguese.

In the middle of the game he began to nod off, like one of those nodding dogs you used to see in the rear window of utility vehicles in the 1970s, and he decided it would be better to lie down and rest. Tomorrow would be another day of work and solitude, of starting, perhaps, to dictate his first version into the tape recorder. Now the best thing was to sleep. Say goodnight to Lucretius. Say goodnight to the sea and go to bed. Forget about all the problems and sleep like a maraca-playing angel, generous and rhythmic.

8

It was around two months since he had heard the diagnosis
of the ophthalmic condition that would condemn him to
blindness in no more than six months, and to having to
complete his translation of *Ensaio sobre a Cegueira* as
quickly as possible. Days earlier, a week or ten days at
most, Francis had visited the eye doctor. He had decided
to carry on seeing the same insensitive ophthalmologist
who had so brutally revealed his destiny as a blind man
with no known cure. His decision was the result of
careful reflection. If it was true that for someone like
him – brought up in a different society: not better or
worse, just different – the doctor's explanation of his
illness, its origin, its evolution and shattering diagnosis,
had made something of an impression, then perhaps that
devastating frankness, no holds barred, was characteristic
of Protestant Anglo-Saxon societies with a very different
understanding of charity. Anyway, given that it was a
degenerative illness, acute but progressive, nobody
could have a better idea of the patient's progress than
the man who had carried out the first tests and analyses

and then ventured a diagnosis. Ventured. He repeated that word like a mantra. Ventured. Ventured. Ventured with no certainty.

The first symptoms – a discreet defensive reaction or photophobia, which manifested on particularly sunny days, the norm over there, and which gave him unbearable and incapacitating migraines, and a progressive tendency to see worms floating in front of his eyes, located at the outer limits of his field of vision (something they call photopsia) – had given way to the sense that he was losing vision at what had previously been the outer limits of his perception. It was as if he had a central image that was still clear and perfectly defined, but starting to fade at the edges. A sort of bifocalism or restricted field of vision. This setback didn't stop him from leading an almost normal life, but, at times, he had to turn his head a little to the left or right in order to focus on things that were a few degrees beyond the central axis. It was as if his ability to glance sideways had been totally destroyed. He couldn't explain it very well, maybe because nobody had bothered to explain to him how one goes about losing one's sight and the different stages of deterioration.

At the beginning he bore it somewhat phlegmatically, given the slow progress of the disability. He compared this slowness with the swift way in which the protagonists of the novel he was translating lost their sight. That gave him the impulse – he couldn't really say why, but it did – to believe that he would finish the translation before losing his sight altogether and anyway, he deceived himself, the development of medical therapies was so rapid that they might very well discover the cure for his condition before his loss of sight became irreversible. They were illusions in a life that, in some ways, was petering out, disappearing into an endless tunnel, black with the black of night and the black of death.

The ophthalmologist, a chilly Aryan, descended from a family of nineteenth-century German pioneers, received him more warmly than expected. He knew of Francis's liking for literature, which he confessed to sharing, and when he said, "I'm going to measure your field," he added, considering himself rather droll, "nothing to do with Kafka's surveyor." The joke, which only Dr Wassermann considered such, for in truth it wasn't very funny, deserved something more than a smile, so the doctor gave a self-sufficient roar of laughter. Francis thought that the ophthalmologist's humour was pretty poor, or not particularly funny, but he went along with it and laughed, discreetly and without overdoing it, at Dr Wassermann's comment.

The results of the doctor's measurement of Francis's field of vision were as expected. In reality they simply provided a numerical statement of Francis's own perception of the bilateral lack of focus he was experiencing in his field of vision. Dr Wassermann talked about a 23% loss of field of vision and an opacity of 10% at the internal limits. This didn't really affect Francis very much, since he thought in less numerical terms and believed in things that couldn't be measured. And also, Dr Wassermann added, during the detailed eye examination he had discovered an inflammation in the arterioles of the retina – "retinitis," he said drily to reaffirm the explanation or to introduce a technical term that marked the difference between them – which was going to make him hypersensitive to sunlight. He strongly recommended Francis use dark glasses – "the sort blind singers might wear on stage," he said, feeling alternately ingenious and then rather uncomfortable with the tragicomic connotations – and avoid exposure to the sun like the plague. Francis reacted well, thanking him for the information and wrote out the cheque before he was asked. The doctor, with dignity and a certain chill, indicated that Francis should pay the nurse, as he left, since she dealt with the finances.

He left the appointment with a couple of prescriptions for eye drops to be picked up from the pharmacy, some vitamin pills and a note for the optician, which specified the thickness and degree of opacity required for his protective lenses. He also had a reactive depression in his back, which, after climbing up his spine, settled on the back of his neck, making him nauseous whenever he turned his head. Past and future images passed through his head in hysterical succession, with horrifying flashbacks. He didn't really know why, but his mind was filled with images of asylums full of madmen twirling repeatedly around a column. Hours and hours until their strength was exhausted. Automatic and without any stimulus. Twisting and turning, never stopping, looking only at the base of the column, destroyed, lost forever, alienated in their lack of feeling, of a vital compass, their immense emptiness. The image of Dr Wassermann assaulted him. He imagined him happy in his arrogance, making love with the nurse, dressed in leather and receiving a thrashing with a whip, sweating and salivating before the sado-nurse with her sardonic smile and the attributes of an excessive, fecund

Valkyrie. This got a definite and comforting smile out of him, which was no small achievement.

Once outside, he looked up at the sky and felt the dagger of the sun tearing into his eyes. It was five in the afternoon and the sun was setting as usual over the San Francisco streets. He walked to the parking lot to pick up the blue convertible and get the hell out of there, back to the beach house, his umbilical retreat, where shelter and the comfort of familiar territory awaited him, along with an unfinished project.

He got into the car and shifted gears in his mind. He needed to be doing things, to be busy all day, to work continuously and hurry up with the translation. The progress of his condition was scientifically demonstrated – that 23% which would soon reach 40%, 50% and so on until the light was completely extinguished. The verdict was there, cold sentence and cruel destiny, and the countdown, irredeemably and dramatically, had begun.

On the way he was planning to drop into the pharmacy and the optician's. Despite the depression, or perhaps to frighten it off, he had to buy the prescriptions as soon as possible, cut short the progress of the disease, eliminate or minimize the most painful symptoms. He put on a tape by Los Van Van and continued his journey until he dropped anchor in Peter's bar. Martin often stopped there on the way home from work and Francis decided to go in, to see if he could talk to him and update him on the progress of the project. He could have telephoned, but it would be better this way, so Martin could see him with his own eyes, still useful for work and talking enthusiastically about the positive progress of the job he'd been assigned. He was out of luck. Martin wasn't there. At this time of day an elegant man wouldn't drink a vodka Martini, but he wasn't an elegant man and he would be even less of one when he was wearing his dark glasses, the glasses of a hereditary blind man or a photophobic writer.

Peter wasn't working behind the bar, so he couldn't count on the support of a friendly ear. The barman who served him his mixer was a lad with an Amerindian face and perhaps a complex about his Mexican origins, since he replied in an almost perfect English when Francis said something to him in Spanish about the result of the Padres' last baseball game. The conversation was brief and rather uncomfortable for both of them, and the barman cut it off immediately with the excuse of a phone call. Those young barmen weren't very professional, thought Francis, they didn't know how to treat a longstanding customer, familiarly, but without overdoing it, attentively, but without insisting too much, listening patiently and giving textbook advice, without risky theories, and cheering up the customer, who if he was treated well would always return to drop anchor in the sheltering port. After this thought, Francis decided to call Rose, to see about having dinner together and catching up on what had been going on.

When he got home he was barely in the mood to cook. He was overcome by an apathy and indolence uncharacteristic of someone usually so tranquil and serene. He would order some tortillas from the Mexican restaurant by the beach. He opened a bottle of Lambrusco, to cheer himself up a bit and calm down, to whet his appetite and relax before Rose arrived, which wouldn't be long now. He had a sip and felt better. He left the top off the bottle. It would improve with oxidation and with time, he thought, as he sat down on the sofa and dialled the restaurant.

Rose was splendid, with her nut-brown vest revealing her belly button and her matching shorts giving way to a pair of outstanding hips, the hips of an elastic young female, a gazelle or a heron, a woman trained in dance classes, ballet shoes and tutus, a fixed barre and many repetitions.

She scrutinized him as if foreseeing a tragedy to be resolved, as if predicting a moral defeat to be overcome, to be pushed aside, to be laid waste with a little affection and wild sex. In two strides she came over to Francis and gave him a magnificent kiss, in close-up and like a sweeping camera shot, from the end of a 1950s film, of the cruel and shameless woman swiftly moving in for a feline assault and a direct attack on the prisoner's jugular.

They fell to the floor and without being conscious of it were already tearing off their clothes, with no rituals or method, with the skill of experienced lovers, lustfully impulsive and moving swiftly into action. From the first anxious kisses on neck and lips, cheeks and forehead, they moved on to nibbles on the ear and intense embraces, until after a succession of games and charges they lay beside one other, panting slowly and gasping with difficulty. It was the typical intensity of Rose and Francis's meetings. Afterwards they calmed down and took everything more steadily, but the first assault was always decisive, persecution and defeat, a fleeting encounter, like sex in the bathrooms at work.

Just a few minutes after the assault was over, a miracle of coordination and mobile phoning, the delivery guy from the Mexican restaurant called at the door and greeted them with the price of the tortillas in two languages (*buenas noches / good evening, señor*) to see if he would score a tip with which to supplement his emigrant's salary. He was polite (*aquí tiene, señor, sus tortillas de pollo con jalapeño / here it is, sir, your chicken tortillas with jalapeño sauce. Enjoy your meal / buenas noches, mister*) and Francis couldn't deny him a reward in the form of two dollar bills and a goodbye (*buenas noches / good night*), which brought him back to the reality of the semi-cold or nearly warm tortillas, too spicy or rather insipid, depending on one's taste and perception.

They ate with wild enjoyment, forgetting they had a bottle of Lambrusco resting on the kitchen table. Only just before finishing the tortillas did Francis go to find the wine and two glasses. There was no special reason to celebrate, so they decided to raise their glasses to happiness and the future, to peace and prosperity, commonplaces in that well-worn discourse, at times so far from reality, where peace and prosperity are really markers of class and only exist for the lucky few.

The conversation was frank and rather tense, as it so often is when one is discussing realities and projects, reflecting on life and wagering on the future. Francis's sight was deteriorating, slowly but irrefutably. He needed a change of climate, to get out of that excessive California, with all its sun and its high-speed everything, all that pressure at work and so little peace and quiet to concentrate on the translation. The job, in contrast to his illness, was progressing much more quickly than normal, with many hours at his desk, seldom leaving the house except for rare walks on the beach.

Rose thought the best thing for Francis was to go back to the family home, which had belonged to his grandparents, where he would be able to work without interruptions and where he would be looked after if more complications arose. His nephew Clodio lived there, accompanied only by Zoe, a very clever and very friendly bitch. Clodio had been over to visit about two years back and had said again and again that the house was at Francis's disposal whenever he wanted to pay a visit.

There was no argument. Francis had thought about it many times and even hinted once or twice, repeatedly but discreetly, mining the terrain like an expert sapper. He needed a change of air, of climate and workplace, to flee the suffocation of closely-watched liberty, of subtle but constant pressure. He had always liked to work under pressure, as long as it was a self-imposed pressure, according to his own strict timetable, full of self-control and clear milestones, which he set for himself. He was certainly prepared for that, but not for the psychological pressure of constant telephone calls and requirements, of permanent oversight, people coming and going in and out of his scheduled routine, reducing his voluntarily-established rhythm to ashes. Furthermore, Clodio was a peaceful and very discreet lad and it would be very easy – he spoke from experience – to live with him. Francis also supposed that Luisa, Clodio's girlfriend, would be a quiet and organized girl; her main interest being entomology, she shouldn't in principle be a strident or difficult woman.

They swiftly agreed, after a short and friendly negotiation, where each clearly expressed both his desires and the real possibilities – that permanent contradiction between reality and desire – that Francis would travel immediately to Padrón, to his family home, and that Rose would visit him after four or five weeks, whenever she could request a vacation week from the consultancy. Now all he had to do was make the appropriate phone calls, get the ticket and think positive, without drama or protracted deliberation, without moral blackmail or tears.

Rose didn't know Clodio other than through the positive things she had heard, both from Francis and from Francis's friends, who had met him on his visit to California, but although she wanted to go with Francis, she couldn't travel right now, because of the limited vacations she had in the company where she worked and because of the urgency to finish the project she was currently assigned to.

That obsession with her career, thought Francis, was going to affect her health, she was already very nervous and very tense. There was nothing for it. Francis would have to go on his own. Maybe in a couple of months, or even before – although this didn't depend only on her, but on the progress of the project she was working on with other people – she would be able to ask for two weeks off to visit him and cheer him up a bit, but now it was impossible.

"You'll have to go on your own, my love. You know very well that it'd be grand to go with you. To get to know your country, you've talked about it so often and it sounds so much like Ireland, although I can't quite believe that. And to meet Clodio, who you've talked about so much as well. He must be a very smart and gorgeous fella."

"I don't know about smart, but gorgeous runs in the family," Francis joked. "He wants to meet you too. A while back, when I told him we were going out together, he sent me an e-mail saying he should have met you by now. Youthful impulse, you know."

"Yes, you told me. I should have met him by now too."

"Well, we'll have to get it all organized. The plane ticket, the bank accounts so I have some funds over there, saying goodbye to my friends... By the way, I'll have to make a stop in Chicago. It's ages since I saw Andy. The guy doesn't even come and visit when he spends the weekend in San Francisco. I haven't seen him since last Christmas, when you and I went to Chicago, and I want to see him, I miss him. You know. It's a good excuse. A stopover in Chicago on the way to Madrid. Also, if I go with the same airline, there won't be many problems with choosing a timetable or making reservations."

"Yes, it's a grand idea. Andy'll be pleased to see you, he's been really worried about his friend Aldo's amphetamine addiction."

"It's not amphetamines. It's an addiction to methamphetamine, or what they call *ice, chalk, crystal, glass* and lots of other things you'd know if you listened out on the street."

"OK, let's not argue over stupid things now. It'll be better if you pick up the phone and start making the calls you have to make."

"You're right, but we'd better drink some of the Lambrusco that's still left. Then I'll start getting organized, but I'm thirsty."

The tortillas were really good and there was no complaint on those grounds. Andy wasn't at home, so Francis decided to boot up the computer and send a few messages: to Andy, at his work address, and to Clodio, so close through virtual contact. It was late and not the best time to call the airline. Tomorrow he would call the American-Airlines booking office to get a ticket from San Francisco to Santiago via Chicago and Madrid. Now it was time to curl up at home or to take a walk on the beach. The temperature was mild and there was a full moon that invited anything but staying indoors, staring at each other like idiots. Rose agreed and they went out to walk beneath the moonlight, to splash around in the water and be caressed by the sounds of the waves. Delightful.

9

The idea had been Rose's. To have a farewell party so that Francis could enjoy the company of his closest friends before crossing the Atlantic to take refuge in the house of his ancestors, the umbilical sanctuary where all the memories of his self-mythologized childhood were concentrated, along with the genetic labyrinths of his ancestry.

At first Francis had reacted less than well, saying that it wasn't right, that he was planning to be back in three or four months, that farewell parties disheartened him, plunged him into a reactive depression, made him feel there was something definitive or deadly about his trip.

"You have a party when there is a reason for it," he had said, transgressing his own behavioural norm and scandalously contradicting his own usual practice, "not when somebody is going away to work on a translation of a novel, which is a ridiculous reason for a party. I do not see the need to stand on ceremony, to dodge around the most elaborate hypocrisies."

"Don't be lazy. Your friends love you a lot. Don't ask me why – I'm already beginning to wonder whether you have any friends with any sense at all – but they love you a lot. You'd better believe it."

"Alright. They love me a lot and I love them, but we do not have a party every time they go to give a lecture in Saint Paul or New Orleans, or when it occurs to one of them to go and do a report on the Atacama Desert for *National Geographic*, to give just two examples of my dear, globetrotting friends."

"Look, Francis, pet, I don't want to be mean, but you're not leaving me any choice. Your friends want to talk to you, so you can see them for the last time before… before you go blind."

There followed one of those pauses when some say an angel passes by. This one lasted long enough for two angels. Suddenly Rose got her voice back and said:

"I thought that's how you would feel. Maybe I was wrong. I'm sorry. I'm really sorry."

"No. Don't be sorry. It's better you say what you think. I'm struggling with these feelings every day, every hour, every minute of my life. You can't imagine what it is to think 'this is the last time I will walk along Portola Drive and be able to see the blue hibiscus I like so much,' or 'this is, without a doubt, the last time I will be able to read these lines from Borges,' or 'this could be the last time I will see a dolphin leap in Santa Barbara Bay, or that I will be able to stand ecstatic in front of a Georgia O'Keeffe painting, or…' It's a constant obsession and you want to sacralize it so I can see my friends, one by one, as if they were specimens from a museum of curiosities. I like Georgia O'Keeffe's paintings and walking along Portola Drive, and looking at the blue hibiscus, and being able to sit on a rock in Santa Barbara Bay, reading one of Borges's 'conjectural' poems, and being able to look up and see a spotted dolphin or a school of tuna crossing the near horizon in the twilight of golden reflections or beneath the shining, happy moon."

"I didn't want to hurt your feelings, Francis. I only want you to be happy, to go to Galicia with the knowledge that you'll come back different, that it's going to be a journey of change, of beginnings, if you prefer, but that when you come back, we'll all be here, waiting for you. I only want you to be happy and that's why I tried…"

"You're right, Rose, I'm sorry. I've been a bit nervy for the last few days. You're absolutely right. I need to shake off this sadness and confront the reality that is submerging me a little more each day, which makes me shudder just to think about the future. All of you – especially you, Rose – are here to help me, I know, but I'm still not up to coming to terms with what my future will be. I wanted it to be different and less programmed, open and not so damn dark."

"OK. I'm glad you're being a bit less stubborn, coming back down to earth and managing to get things into perspective, it'll just be a normal act of friendship and camaraderie, not a hypocritical and unfeeling celebration. We really do love you, Francis. We know it's a hard test you're about to go through and we're here, believe me, to help as much as we can."

Francis nodded and smiled back at her. She – Rose – always had that generous smile, full of considered satisfaction and the joy of living. It was very typically Irish, this tendency to conceal the most profound sadness beneath a patina of pneumatic happiness and resignation. The skill of those accustomed to suffering, thought Francis, always pondering how to face up to misfortune.

The sound of the telephone ripped through the nirvana of smiles and complicity, of long-distance caresses and routine activity, of the harmonious life of a long-term couple. It was Andy, calling from Milwaukee. It was Monday and he had just picked up Francis's e-mail announcing his stopover on the Friday. He was calling to say yes, that he would be waiting at Chicago airport, not to worry, Francis was aware of just how complicated his life was, three days a week in Milwaukee, two days in Chicago and travelling every other weekend to San Francisco to be with Aldo, his most recent lover. Andy said all this to Rose, without stopping for formalities, ploughing through his speech until the end. Rose was measured and knew to listen to the thousandth complaint about a long-promised, even planned visit to Chicago, which she skilfully dodged by passing the phone to Francis who was soon engaged in a code-ridden conversation with good old Andy, so loyal and such a good conversationalist, so enthusiastic and so little given to limits.

Rose waved goodbye from the door.

"I'm going to buy some things for the party, charcoal for the grill, drinks and burgers. You know Martin only eats meat. Back soon," she waved goodbye and closed the door carefully, leaving Francis on the phone.

Francis carried on talking to Andy about Aldo's problems with methamphetamine, a terrible drug that was changing his character, making him aggressive and with little respect for anybody else, even Andy. Then he saw Rose through the window going over to the blue convertible, reordering the kinetics of her voluptuous body pounded in the mortar of constant sex, walking with the perfect rhythm of a contemporary dancer, those marvellous, near-perfect beings. He fell silent for a moment and let Andy carry on talking. About how he loved him a lot. How sorry he was they hadn't seen each other more. His problems and worries, his struggle to pull Aldo out of his drugs hell and his grief at the loss of his mother, so fragile towards the end and so essential for Andy's emotional stability. In this way, not really listening, letting Andy's conversation flow, Francis thought how lucky he had been to meet Rose, such a real woman, which had gone some way towards compensating for Andy's romantic withdrawal, Andy, his first American lover, his first passionate surprise, when he was still so young and had so many doubts. Fortunately Andy would always be there, no longer a sexual object, but a friend forever, no longer a lover, but loyal guardian of their memories and secrets. There was no need for Rose to know the details of what had happened between them, how deep they had sunk and how far their desire had taken them. It would be – already was – his best-kept secret.

"It's OK, Andy. See you on Friday at O'Hare."

"I'll be there, Francis. I'll be there. We could go for dinner at a restaurant I know, near North Clark Street and then…"

"It's OK, Andy. It's OK. We will talk about it when I get to Chicago. Or better, you will make plans and surprise me. You know I prefer surprises to well-organized plans. Look after yourself. See you on Friday."

"Good bye, Francis."

"See you, Andy. Take care of yourself."

Francis had had to cut him off at the end of the conversation. Andy could go on forever on the phone. It was his favourite means of seduction. Talking endlessly, unrestrainedly, weaving the conversation around until he mesmerized his interlocutor. He was a good guy, Andy, rather hyperkinetic and too focused on his work, but a good friend, loyal like few others. He would keep their secret and never tell Rose what had happened between them. Not Rose, not Aldo, not anybody.

Francis started work. He sat down in front of the computer and turned on the word processor where he had already saved the first draft that somebody from the publisher's office had transcribed for him from the tapes he had recorded at home. He began to work through the pages, which he already considered semi-definitive. He printed out seven or eight of them, which would be his job for the day, and began to work through them with a fine toothcomb. First quickly, in case he found a typo or error of syntax, then sentence by sentence, to try out the sound and rhythm, reading aloud, as he usually did when correcting, then finally word by word, trying to find the most appropriate synonyms, if he found some word that didn't sound right in the context, or that didn't come easily given Saramago's kind of writing, so richly nuanced and with such a precise vocabulary. He spent two or three hours on this, reading the pages again and again until his gaze burned into them, until they had suffered through corrections and recorrections and were unrecognizable, full of crossings-out and alternative text scribbled in the margins, in a tiny hand, illegible to anybody but himself, and even then, sometimes, he wasn't sure exactly what they said. Lucretius visited now and again for a stroke, but after being pushed away for the second time, he realized Francis wasn't in the mood for play and left him alone for the rest of the afternoon.

Around seven o'clock, Rose came back with the car full of meat and other bits and pieces. Francis couldn't believe the amount of things that emerged from the blue convertible.

"I let you use the car and you bring it back full up like a delivery wagon."

"You wouldn't want your guests to go hungry."

"Of course not. I'm just surprised that such a small car can hold so much stuff."

"It's a question of organization," said Rose, heading for the kitchen to get things going.

"Let me help. You know I love being in the kitchen," said Francis, coming in with a couple of bags that Rose had left in the trunk.

"Don't even think about it, sweetheart. You're a great cook, sure you are. But today you're the guest of honour. Like it or not, you're one of the guests. Or rather, you're the most important guest, so don't even think about setting foot in the kitchen. Sanctum sanctorum, forbidden territory, *vedado, interdite, vervooden*. Katty and Paul will be here soon to help me get everything ready. You just pour yourself a drink and relax."

"As you wish, but at least let me light the grill. Did you get the charcoal?"

"Yes," Rose said. "It's in the back of the car."

As Rose had predicted, Katty and Paul were the first to arrive. Francis was in the garden getting the grill going so it was Rose who went out to greet them as soon as she heard their car driving on to the gravel track at the front of the house. Katty worked at the University of San Diego, in the English department, and she and Francis had taken a postgraduate course together. Since then they had enjoyed a distant but respectful friendship, a rather formal friendship with few breaks. Her boyfriend and future husband, by the looks of things, and because they had said so on a previous occasion, was Paul, a marine biologist who had always worked, at least since he graduated, in the main lab of the Scripps Institution of Oceanography in La Jolla, handling statistics on the accidental capture of dolphins by boats fishing for tropical tuna. A rather routine office job, just statistics and tables, histograms of frequencies, temporal series and the odd correlation, but dangerous as far as data collection ever was, thanks to the economic interests involved and the possible sanctions. He was still talking about tuna cartels, multinational business organizations, who didn't hesitate to fund ecological campaigns to stamp out certain fishing techniques used by their rivals, who bought governments, sold favours and bribed international observers, who influenced their respective governments, even going so far as to defenestrate the odd minister or undersecretary.

Rose accompanied them out to the garden, where they had put two tables in the welcoming shade of a royal poinciana with orange flowers and elongated branches. They had brought two bottles of wine to add to the arsenal of drinks prepared for the party: Mexican beer and Labatt Blue, Polish vodka, white Martini, dark rum, wine from the Napa and Sonoma Valleys, cartons of mango, pineapple, Florida orange, guava and papaya juice. On the other table, Rose had begun to place ready-made dishes ordered from the Whole-Foods supermarket, snow crab, essential at a celebration like this, Pacific salmon with herbs, escabeche of eel, sea-urchin eggs, marinated Chinese mushrooms, black olives, dried squid, Pang-Kheo tofu, Indian peaches, California clams, gooseberry compote, smoked halibut in a crab-egg sauce, pork cutlets with honey and other treats which they would serve on the side with the grilled fish and meat that Francis had just got going.

They had barely started up the usual conversation about the weather and how good the food was looking, going from one surprise to another, savouring the thought of the flavours to come and exchanging commonplaces and endless anecdotes, when Martin arrived with his new lover, a spectacular blonde, who could have been taken for his daughter and who dethroned his former lovers, including the dolphin-loving, eco-conscious secretary with whom he now shared only the administrative chores at the publisher's.

Martin wandered over to Francis to find out about the progress of the coals, the quality of the meat, and the state of mind of his friend / colleague / employee / translator / associate editor, who was at the bottom of the garden trying to work up a suitably large fire. Martin's lover, on her own initiative, joined in Paul and Katty's conversation, handing over some flowers of dubious taste and a bottle of French champagne that Rose hurried off to the kitchen to make sure it was properly chilled.

Aldo, Andy's lover, parked his 4x4 by the side of the road (there wasn't any more room behind the house) and got out of the car, nervy and very talkative, going to embrace Rose, to pick her up, to kiss her enthusiastically while he looked over the guests and scoped out the territory.

Rose's female friends were trickling in gradually. Some of her office mates (two Irish, one Chinese) and other (two nurses, a journalist) university friends who she was still close to. Rui came too, bringing CDs of Brazilian music to liven up the party – some batucadas, some Chico Science & Nação Zumbi – and Dougal, who worked as a photographer for *National Geographic*, just back from Greenland (still rather stunned from the change of temperature and light), and who was planning to record the event for posterity.

A kind of dance started up as people moved from one group to another, talking and exchanging greetings and congratulations, news of activities and more or less standard questions, as they drank beer or juice, mixers or wine, depending on their preferences or boundaries. Then Huo arrived with a plastic bag containing two snappers for the grill and a bottle of sake. Francis made a special effort to greet him, trying to make sure he felt part of the group as soon as possible and didn't experience any kind of distance.

Rui immediately got along with Aldo. Huo easily fell into conversation with Rose's Chinese friend and, of course, now he would have a new, regular client at his fishmonger's. The nurses were all getting on together in all possible areas, and Martin started a conversation with Katty about Hispanic literature, to the despair of the incredible blonde, who couldn't really follow the conversation and had to be content with talking to one of Rose's friends about diets and gyms, infusions and restorative syrups. Dougal and Paul didn't take long to start imagining reportage projects, which they might follow up or not, but which helped them to get to know each other better and for there to be a possibility of collaboration. Everybody was defending and marking out territories, eating here and there, this and that, a bit of fish and a bit of literature, Brazilian music and cutlets with honey, a bit of Marxism and red wine, some politics with snow crab, mixed conversations and escabeche of eel, natural disasters and mango juice, politics, economics and tofu, random literary anniversaries (these always came up, filled all the available time, pandered to nostalgia, kept the cultural world focused on the past, and, all in all, were something of a plague) and smoked halibut, German sausages and Latin funk, dirty jokes and more vodka Martini, plastic surgery and grilled snapper, exotic trips and guava juice, eyes meeting, musical interludes, canticles, toasts and farewells. They spoke of a huge range of subjects, but nobody at any point, whether out of politeness or omission, mentioned blindness.

In the end people left in groups (Rose's friends in one group, Paul, Katty and Dougal in another), in pairs (the nurses, Rui and Aldo, Martin and the imposing blonde) or disappointedly alone (Rose's Chinese friend, the journalist), in a disorder of new friendships or simply collusions, of treasure troves of accumulated glances that opened the door to new experiences or with the tedium reflected in under-eye bags, from eating and drinking too much.

Huo stayed until the end. He had agreed with Francis that he would take care of Lucretius. A fishmonger's would be the ideal place for a cat and, furthermore, Rose couldn't look after him as she was very busy and her San Francisco apartment didn't have room for a cat. Huo was radiant, he had dared to ask the Chinese girl he had met at the party for her number. For sure, she had gone a step further and invited him to dinner, on Saturday, to talk and get to know each other better. She had said all this in Mandarin, which meant even more to him. He was radiant and very sweet, as if the girl's eyes had breathed new life into him. He hugged Francis so tight he almost squeezed him to death and promised to treat Lucretius like a prince.

Rose and Francis were left alone, looking at the stars from beneath the poinciana, surrounded by a mess they didn't really feel like clearing up. From indoors the loudspeakers were pumping out the cheerful, bubbling-toned, infinitely-nuanced voice of Elis Regina, who was singing *Nada será como antes*, or "nothing will be as it was," by Milton Nascimento and Ronaldo Bastos. They were alone, embracing at the beach house and dreaming of an imperfect future. They were silent, keeping each other company and drinking wine, looking at the stars and the waves breaking on the beach, whispering and filling the beach with phosphorescence. In two days Francis would leave for the other side of the Atlantic and nothing would be as it was, and Elis would sing *qualquer dia a gente se vê... que notícias me dâo de você?... que nada sera como antes... amanhã... qualquer dia a gente se vê...* and his voice mingled with the waves or the breeze, with the passing of time and the lost glances of the lovers... *nothing will be as it was... tomorrow...*

10

The farewell party had been the previous night. Today had been a quieter day, socially, with fewer interactions and fewer goodbyes, but plenty of preparations and countless last-minute emergencies, as always happens when one is about to undertake a journey for an indeterminate but lengthy period, a stay rather than a holiday. At last they managed to get all the necessities– which they had got down to just the barest necessities – together in a single suitcase. Francis figured he could definitely do without most of the clothing Rose was encouraging him to take, so after some minor arguments (minor in both intensity and consequences) they had decided he was fully kitted out. There were also last-minute chores to be sorted out, like a note to ask the mailman to keep all Francis's correspondence at the post office, from where Rose would take it upon herself to collect it once a week, going to say goodbye to Lucretius, who would be looked after by Huo, and a message asking the *San Francisco Chronicle* to freeze his subscription for an indefinite period, and to arrange for him to receive the

Sunday edition in Galicia so as not to fall out of touch with news from the US and the city.

That afternoon they hadn't done anything special; they had taken a walk on the beach, had a brief romantic interlude, taken a spur-of-the-moment siesta and dined frugally in front of the television.

It was almost one in the morning when, after watching the umpteenth rerun of a Bogart film – from back when films were remembered for the star and not so much for the director – they cleared the table, emptied the ashtrays and the glasses, scraped the leftovers from the plates, and headed for the bedroom.

"Tomorrow we must be up early," said Francis, swallowing his anxiety at the idea.

"The airport's not far. No need to be so serious, you slugabed," said Rose as she wriggled down beneath the covers.

"Are you not going to read?" asked Francis.

"No. I'm knackered."

Rose certainly must have been tired, because no more than two minutes later she was singing out a melody somewhere around seventh heaven, that strange place where sleep is deeper and more comforting. Francis set the alarm on his clock radio to wake him up with music at 7 a.m. He flicked through a current affairs magazine, *Detour*, which he bought for the pleasure of another routine, for no particular reason except perhaps – he guessed – to avoid buying *Newsweek* or *Forbes*, whose rancid US nationalism he found unbearable. After a while, he turned out the light and thought about how good it would feel to get off to sleep quickly, since he would have to be up early tomorrow. But Francis was not made of the same stuff as Rose and sleep didn't come easily, so he got out of bed and went over to the living-room window for a smoke and a think, to look at the San Rafael sea, brilliantly phosphorescent, and to think about Andy. Recently he was smoking more than usual, almost a packet a day. He made a firm decision to cut down as he sucked on the stub for longer than was advisable. The day had been an intense one of events and phone calls. He was exhausted but his disquiet overcame his physical exhaustion. He looked out of the window at the immense sea leaving its waves on the San Rafael sands. A canticle like a permanent lullaby. Thousands and thousands of times, for countless years, for aeons (maybe he was exaggerating), the sea had left its waves on the San Rafael sands and it would continue to do so for thousands and thousands more years. Thinking of this increased his disquiet, his feeling of insignificance and misery. What must those lands have been like a hundred, a thousand, ten thousand years ago? Who could have been the first person to leave a footprint on the beach that now stretched out before his house? Would it have been a man, or maybe a bear or an otter coming down the river into the sea? Would it have been a native woman? Native of where? A woman of what race? What ethnicity? A girl or an adult woman? What about a man like him, come from the other side of the world? Perhaps an Asian migrant – Mongol or Samoyed – or a Cheyenne, a Sioux or an Arapahoe, enraged and brutal?

Francis didn't feel at all sleepy and missed Lucretius, who, had he been there, would have answered any call.

Solitude transmits a certain texture to the atmosphere, something not easily defined but which settles itself in the air and invades it with pheromonal efficiency. Lucretius knew that very well, and always came when Francis called, automatically and without any hesitation, to scratch away Francis's solitude, to scratch away his own, to mingle solitudes.

The day dawned, covered with a blanket of clouds. Francis awoke with unusual energy, perhaps due to the immediate realization that today was not a day for work, but for travel, not for routine, but for re-encounters, not such a bad day after all, and that, thinking about it, the clouds would give way to the sun, and that the clouds themselves were glittering, beautiful in their cumulus state, their Magrittean whiteness against a background of sky blue, jellyfish blue, the blue of eyes desired and close.

Rose stretched out like a heron doing its morning stretching exercises, expansively and placidly, like a swan, unfurling its neck and shaking out its wings. Francis looked out some lively music by Machito and his Afro-Cubans with their magnificent versions of *Sopa De Pichon* and *Quimbombo*, filling the whole house with Caribbean rhythms and delirious percussion, with incomprehensible choruses and a craving for a mango smoothie.

After a super-quick shower – get in, get wet, get soaped, get wet, get dry – they were ready for a super-quick breakfast – bottled orange juice, coffee with ginger cookies and a slice of bread with butter and strawberry jam – and a meticulous check through the necessary items – passport, plane ticket, credit cards, suitcase and hand luggage with the basics for the layovers – and then ready to jump in the blue convertible and head out along the south road to the airport where Francis would catch his American Airlines flight to Chicago.

They got to the airport just in time, with no chance to meander through the gift stores: a pack of cigarettes for Andy, who had smoked Marlboro Lights since forever, a Paul Auster novel and a baseball cap for Clodio, who was waiting for him in Galicia with open arms and an enormous house where he would be able to work in peace and rediscover the past and his roots, some chocolates for Luisa, who – however much of an entomologist she was – would surely like sweets.

At the airport it was a very emotional farewell, with many hugs and caresses. They embraced each other closely, with the intensity of knowing they were saying goodbye for a long time, with a shared feeling of physical distance and emotional proximity, of consensual separation and a need to reflect on the future.

Rose had one of those cameras that can be hooked up to the computer to look at photos. As soon as she could she would e-mail the photos, she said, trying to raise his spirits, while Francis showed his boarding pass to the American Airlines women and went through Gate 17 on his way to the plane that would carry him to Chicago.

When they looked at each other for the last time it was just briefly, as if each of them wanted to keep the other's image in their memory forever, with no conditions and no feelings of blame or desire. A gaze without prejudice and at the same time as humble, as empty of emotion and feeling as if the separation were a liberation, a lapse of behaviour, a relief for a couple whose relationship had been fractured and worn down by events and by the recent accumulation of doubts. Francis's condition had given the relationship a great deal of focus, adding intense analysis and bringing them closer in a relatively short period of time. The normal thing for a couple who had been together barely nine months was lots of sex, little reflection, an imaginary intimacy and a great many stories, told in many different ways. The lies that help love survive, the lies that strengthen a relationship torn apart from reality, from the purely physical, to penetrate the arena of fiction or invention. They had forged such a deep friendship, so shaped by its early sensuality, that their future was clearly designed around co-dependency, a stoic union against wind and tide, with little freedom, and total concentration on one another. Their relationship had become life itself, such was its mesmeric, enchanting, amazing character, it nullified any feelings or interactions outside the relationship.

Rose turned brusquely on her heels and walked to the parking lot. As she passed the different airport shops, sadness welled up inside her. She struggled to contain the tears that she had held back so as not to depress Francis, which were falling now in a torrent, in a waterfall, in the tragic pose of a primitive, amphibious Irishwoman. A little boy pointed at her and somebody told him to be quiet. Rose sank into a chair in the lounge and stayed there until her tears ran dry.

Recovering her composure, she sniffed and wiped her eyes, made for the restrooms and composed her face, breathed deeply and let a prolonged sigh expel the sadness from her body. At least for a while. Now she had to carry on living, keep herself busy and not keep dwelling on Francis's condition, Francis's absence, a future she foresaw as imperfect. That night she would make the most of going out with some girlfriends, to occupy her time with other activities where Francis wouldn't be omnipresent, where she could relax and let herself be carried along by trivial conversations, about fashion and the best way to cook tuna, or about the novels they had read and the latest films they had seen, about the boyfriends they had or didn't have, about what they dreamed of at night and stopped dreaming of during the day. She got in the car and listened, humming, to the chorus of a trendy song, looked up at the sky and pressed the button to change the radio station. She ran through several stations with news or advertising – all stories, invented or real. Of course she found a station where they were playing country music. She surprised herself by leaving it on, as she exited the airport on to the road to San Diego, where she had arranged to have dinner and spend the weekend with her lifelong girlfriends. She lit a long cigarette, a Du Maurier, and lowered the roof of the convertible. She loved the sea air. She loved the warm desert wind. She loved the scent from the valleys where the vines grew. She loved everything. There was nothing in the world like living in California, she thought as she watched a succession of beaches and the trees that spattered the countryside whizz past, a scene she so often recreated in her imagination.

Francis soon found his seat, 2C. The seat next to him was empty so that, when they closed the doors, he leaned against the little window and looked out. A stewardess came with a tray of glasses, with champagne or orange juice.

"Would you like a drink before we take off, sir? Champagne? Orange juice?"

"A glass of champagne, thank you," replied Francis with a canned, toothpaste smile, a long way from the worries churning around inside him.

As he thought about the journey, how little he enjoyed travelling by plane, he raised the champagne glass to his lips and looked out of the window. He liked the idea of the champagne. It would make him sleepy and he would feel good, as if he was being carried along in a cloud, free from fear and anxiety.

The stewardess came over again, this time to show him the menu for the journey to Chicago. Meanwhile, the plane began to glide along the runway. He leaned over to the window and looked at the tarmac with his mind blank, watching the runway go past and feeling as if the plane was slipping on the tarmac. It was as if he was travelling in a car and had nothing to fear. He thought of Rose, the last glimpse he had caught of her when they said their understated goodbye, restrained and muted. He also thought of Andy, who would be waiting for him in Chicago. That calmed him.

The journey began well. For reasons he didn't bother to find out, they served dinner immediately, as if the stewardesses wanted to get their work done as soon as possible. The food was a cold buffet, an assortment of smoked fish and various liver pâtés. There were two kinds of bread and the stewardess brought him a little basket so he could choose.

"Some bread, sir?" she said awkwardly, as if realizing the inanity of her question.

"Yes, thank you," Francis replied, not in the mood for detailed conversation.

He took one of each kind of bread, to try. One was a sliced bread with various cereals, where he could smell oats and rye, but also several seeds, here and there, that he couldn't identify. The other was white bread, with an egg wash, its top covered with poppy seeds that fell off easily. That annoyed him a little. Why insist on putting poppy seeds on the bread, if they were just going to drop off at the slightest touch?

Another stewardess – the service was fast and efficient – asked him which wine he would like. There were three kinds – two French whites, and a Californian red that wasn't to be sniffed at. Let his travel companions drink the white! He found white wine gave him bad digestion, especially on planes, with all that fatty, megacalorific food. Who on earth would serve white on aeroplanes? Each to his own. He would treat his palate to that Californian red – a Zinfandel merlot '97– that was recommended in the brochure he had received on boarding.

The smoked fish was very good, very good indeed. First he attacked a slice of delicious Greenland halibut, with a great deal of body and an exquisite hint of American oak, and, of course, he tried the wild salmon (different from farmed salmon in its amount of fat; in smoked fish the difference was even more notable) with a gooseberry compote that had a bitter taste which the tongue savoured, calling for assistance from the Zinfandel. A delight.

The caterers hadn't been very inspired with the choice of pâté and he couldn't go beyond the first bite. The stewardess, who had watched him eat the fish with such great delight, became a little alarmed by his lack of interest in the pâté. Francis gave the faintest hint of an archangelic smile and asked for a little more wine and a little more salmon, if there was any. He sang the praises of the gooseberry compote and the California red and received in exchange a generous portion of salmon with a no less generous quantity of compote.

When the desserts arrived – forest-fruit salad and chocolate cake with nuts – he couldn't resist the temptation to ask for a serving of each and a little more wine to forget once and for all that he was flying, that he had a mass of flying hours to cover and that his eyes were condemned, sentenced to a lingering death, to a slow not-being as he translated a book by a Portuguese writer with enormous glasses, who spoke of blindness, of how we are all blind or gradually become blind until we can see nothing of the world around us, until we are manipulated again and again by those who see, those who govern, those who give orders. The book was an allegory or a parable, or perhaps a game or the madness of a protean and very serious writer whom they talked of for the Nobel Prize despite his communist activism, a little out of step now after the fall of most of the world's Marxist regimes. Perhaps the Portuguese writer – one Saramago, whose name in Portuguese or Galician meant a yellow-flowered weed, growing wild at the roadside, eyes of a millenarian tortoise and body of a quixotic squire, long and rather gangly – would also go blind; like Borges or like Francis himself.

It must have been a long siesta, because he woke up when the stewardess asked him to fasten his seatbelt, as they were coming into Chicago O'Hare. He opened the blind covering the window and was amazed at the immensity of Lake Michigan, with its imprecise edges lapping Chicago's crust, the city of canals, of many bridges, of quays awaiting goods, of emblematic skyscrapers and unpredictable weather. It was raining. It wasn't the rainy season, but it was raining lightly.

II

When Francis got off the plane there were fifteen minutes of airport corridors to navigate before he reached the baggage-reclaim belts. He spotted his suitcase straight away and, with some effort (damn it was heavy!), heaved it on to a trolley. Walking towards the exit, he thought about the real reasons for his visit to Chicago, about how the visit was something of a last glimpse of Andy, of his endless smile, his dear eyes, with their precious mestizo shape, his velvety skin and his penis, indigo like the membranes of his eyes and gums, and he thought, too, how short a time he had left until he saw him, perhaps for the last time. It was scarcely a reason to celebrate, but he made every effort to ensure his face didn't reflect his current state of mind – a deep emotion, a feeling of detachment and distance, as if he was able to see himself from the outside. He strode forward, putting on his best smile so that by the time he passed through the sliding door that led to the meeting point, where relatives, friends and the odd employee brandishing a cardboard sign were waiting for passengers known or unknown, he was displaying his Sunday-best smile, which allowed him to give an impression of determination and light-heartedness.

At first, still a little stunned from the vertiginous descent and the change of pressure that blocked communication between his nose and ears, he couldn't pick Andy out in the waiting crowd. Then, looking closer, he spotted somebody covering his face with a blank piece of white cardboard, like a screen or mimetic mask. It was Andy. He watched him shifting nervously, with his wiry legs and his thin body, and knew immediately that it was Andy who was hiding behind that naive and primitive cardboard camouflage, that nervous pose with an intuitive smile and childish behaviour. He strode briskly towards him. Just as he drew alongside, Andy uncovered his face revealing the little rimless spectacles that barely covered his slanting mixed-race eyes.

The embrace was of the kind that awaken passions where none exist. It lasted so long that Francis felt on the verge of fainting right there in the middle of the airport. Fortunately Andy relaxed his arms and Francis was able regain his breath and his composure.

"I'm so glad you came, Francis. I really am."

"I know. I wouldn't come all the way to Chicago if I didn't think I would be welcome. Let me look at you. You're keeping well, my friend!"

"Let me give you a hand. The car's right here, on the second floor of the parking lot."

"Here you go. Take my hand luggage. The trolley will go better if you take it. Here on the trolley it might slip off the suitcase."

"Hey, how come you didn't check your case in all the way through? It's a hassle to have to carry it from one side to the other."

"It is because of the airlines, the airports and their internal procedures. In San Francisco they told me it wasn't possible, either I had to check it through to Chicago or to Madrid, but all the way to Santiago was impossible, so I decided to check it through to here, because you can help me put it in the car."

"Sure, man, sure. No problem. We'll put it in the car, problem solved," said Andy. "For the six hours you're going to be in Chicago, we might as well leave it in the car."

"Yes, that will be best. Keep the baggage and go and eat something decent in one of those Chinese restaurants you know so well."

Andy nodded and opened the trunk for him. They got in the car – a second-hand Japanese automatic, which immediately huffed to echo their misfortune – and took the beltway to the city centre, between East Monroe and Clark. They went through Dearborn between Washington and Randolph and from there turned north, via North Michigan Avenue and La Salle Drive to Lincoln Park, to get on to North Shore Drive. Andy knew that northern part of the city well, he had bought an apartment there that looked out on to Lake Michigan. It was an area with plenty of life and few problems, a long way from the problem areas of Cabrini Gardens, where the Italians ruled, or the outskirts of Pulaski Park, where the Poles had established their empire, from China Town or the Ukrainian Village. Things had changed a lot since the times of Prohibition and Al Capone, but in certain parts of the city human life still had no value at all. None at all.

When they reached North Halsted, Andy parked the car and said:

"We'll walk from here. The police station's on the corner so we won't have to worry about anything being stolen. Anyhow, this is the quietest area in Chicago, that's why I chose it."

"We are walking?" Francis asked, amazed.

"Yes, we're walking. I want you to see my new neighbourhood. When you and Rose were here during that blizzard, the weather didn't allow for walking. You'll see. It's full of life and colour."

"OK, but I wasn't aware of your liking for walking. When we lived together you took the car everywhere, to buy cigarettes or to get a coffee, to a party or to work, and nobody could get you to break the habit."

"Different times. A guy's gotta evolve."

"I couldn't agree more," Francis agreed. "I'm happy for you. I think I'm evolving in the opposite direction."

They walked along North Halsted. Francis was amazed, it didn't look like a Chicago neighbourhood, at least not one from the harder, wilder Chicago he had known when he was still living with Andy on East Cermak Road, in the heart of Chinatown. This was a model neighbourhood, where you could take a quiet walk and everybody had broad smiles, where you didn't feel as if something bad could happen at any moment, where there were no parking problems or people lying on the streets, drunk on beer or high as a kite on crack or heroin. Crossing West Melrose, they passed a very chic and well-presented restaurant, the Rumba, but Andy said better not. Better to carry on walking for a couple more minutes and go to a Chinese restaurant that Andy visited regularly. A restaurant where they didn't serve food for tourists, but for Chinese families.

It was a good choice. They ordered jellyfish marinated in ginger, oysters in soy sauce and duck legs fried in fat, so crispy and so tasty, which were the most delicious revelation to Francis, unaccustomed in recent years to Chinese cooking other than home-delivery services and the most basic chop sueys.

As soon as they finished their banquet, washed down with two thimbles of sake heated in the bain-marie, they each lit up a cigar. Francis and Andy shared a fondness for Camel and for Marlboro Lights, each with his respective preference, but exchangeable at moments of empty pockets or shared intimacy, ever since the time when they had both been initiated into the art of smoking.

"Smoking in the States is going to turn into a secret vice, like masturbation or calling erotic phone lines," said Andy, as he blew smoke rings with exaggerated enjoyment.

"You're still in luck here in Illinois. In California the situation is really fucked up. Hardly any restaurants have a place for smokers. It's constant persecution, as if we were lepers in the Middle Ages. Hey, you don't need me to tell you this. You must know about it from your trips to San Francisco to see Aldo. It's a disaster."

They carried on talking for an hour as they sipped two thimbles of warm sake and dissected the recent events overshadowing their lives.

Andy's mother had recently died and it had affected him a lot. Francis remembered her, small and slight, sitting in front of a window that looked out over Lake Michigan, watching the boats at the quayside and counting the numbers going in and out with the precision of a lighthouse keeper or port traffic controller. She didn't miss one. She spent whole afternoons watching the birds go by and counting boats, reciting mantras and counting boats, talking to herself and watching the birds go by. When Andy got home she had dinner ready for him and it was always a pleasant surprise, a surprise made with plenty of love and with exquisite care. Andy had felt it deeply. She was great company for him and she helped him survive with dignity and control the times when he had no partner. Andy was a bit out of control when he was single. He fell into the deepest depressions and let himself be carried away by uncontrollable passions, like gambling or drink, wild sex and persistent self-stimulation.

There was no possible consolation, so Francis changed the subject and they began to talk about the problems with his eyesight and the fatal or miraculous coincidence of the project to translate *Ensaio sobre a Cegueira*, how interesting Saramago's work was, especially that particular novel, how blind we all were, the tragedy of having to think it would be the last – if not the very last – time you would do or see or feel something. There was no possible consolation here either, so they decided to declare both subjects – the death of Andy's mother and Francis's blindness – taboo and to go outside for a walk.

"Let's get a coffee somewhere," said Andy, breaking the silence.

"OK. I quite fancied going to the Art Institute. The café is very good and beside I want… I want to say goodbye to some of the rooms. There are paintings I will never…" said Francis, moved.

"We're in luck. Today's the day when it's free to get in and at this time of year there aren't many visitors. Let's go in the car. It'll take fifteen minutes if there are no traffic problems."

They took North Lake Shore Drive as far as North Michigan and from there, after crossing the river, they were at the Arts Institute in a heartbeat. Andy had been right and the entrance hall was almost empty, with no queues or crowds. Just a high school with a pair of enthusiastic teachers and some art students who were taking advantage of the free entry to linger in the rooms with their favourite artists and learn what they didn't teach in school.

As soon as they entered the museum they went straight to the cafeteria (where you could smoke!) and ordered two double espressos to give their spirits a lift. They smoked as they talked over some memories of their shared past, taking care to avoid adding even a drop of bitterness to the difficult times they were remembering. So they remembered only the happiest stories, fragments of a shared life that hadn't always been easy. They remembered that morning when Andy, his head shaved back then and wearing an orange raincoat, was sitting on a stone wall, on the shore of Lake Michigan, breakfasting on a coffee and a muffin and a man came up and asked him if he was a Buddhist and if he was meditating. Andy's response was clear and to the point: "I'm having a coffee and a carrot muffin and I'm neither a Buddhist nor meditating and, if I was, you and your stupid questions would have fucked up my meditation." The man was completely furious and wanted to push him in the lake. Fortunately Andy was quicker and threw the hot coffee in his attacker's face and, as he howled from the pain caused by the coffee, Andy sprinted across Lincoln Park under the watchful gaze of the squirrels. They also recalled the time when there had been a terrible snowstorm, which had paralyzed the city and obliged the mayor to appear on local TV, appealing for calm and assuring people there was enough salt and snowploughs to solve the problem in record time, and they had spent two days trapped in the apartment of some Mexican friends, watching music videos on the Mexican channel Galavisión – quite an experience – and eating tacos delivered by the guy from the restaurant on the corner, who eventually, after three return trips, decided to stay and join the party.

The time had flown by and if they wanted to see something of the museum they would have to hurry. In two hours they had to be at the airport if they were to have enough time to check in the luggage. They climbed the stairs and passed at breakneck speed through all the ancient-art rooms until they reached Kandinsky, who deserved a few minutes' contemplation. From there they went to Room 220, full of paintings by Hubert Robert, with his liking for architecture that combined, with a very particular alchemy, reality (ruins) and desire (reconstruction). There were neoclassical landscapes of temples and columns that always ended in steps lapped by the waves of a sea where you could see triremes and brigs, carracks and other sailing ships. With no time to wallow over their tastes (Francis, Kandinsky; Andy, definitely Hubert Robert), they moved on to Room 248, their favourite – both of theirs – where they admired over and over again the vivid, pure, primitive colours of Georgia O'Keeffe's paintings. They had met in that room, in their youth, when, without knowing why, they had begun a furious discussion full of passion and conflicting arguments. Andy preferred *Red Hills with Flowers*, with a predominance of red, and Francis said the paintings *Green Mountains* or *The Black Place* were much better. They glanced sideways at one another, intensely but sideways, and neither said what he was thinking, but both smiled as if intuiting the other's thoughts.

"I liked *Red Hills with Flowers*, because of the predominance of red, and those discreet yellow brushstrokes on the ends of the petals, and those touches of green at the base of the flowers, and the ochre of the mountains, and the sky, and everything."

"See how complicated you are, Andy, I liked the others just to be contrary, so you wouldn't be right, to see if we'd continue our discussion in the cafeteria and perhaps afterwards in your apartment or mine. God knows how I thanked Georgia O'Keeffe for that meeting!" said Francis, emotionally.

"She was still alive back then. You could have sent her a postcard."

"That would have been a good idea. I could have done that, but I didn't. Now it's too late."

There was a silence that lasted long enough for an angel to pass over, for Andy to reflect on the inexistent or banal reason he had found back then to leave Francis and for Francis to know what Andy was thinking just by gazing into his magnificent eyes, enchanting and tender. A devil must have passed over in pursuit of the angel, because they returned to the conversation and continued their visit. As they walked through other rooms, where they barely stopped, they continued talking over many things that brought them closer and of others that were cooling their relationship, with honesty and affection, as if they were still travelling through life on the same train.

The moment came when Andy couldn't take it any more and all at once he unloaded all of the problems he was having in his relationship with Aldo, who was addicted to methamphetamine and behaving very aggressively. Francis tried to put the problems in context, to play them down, but it was impossible. Aldo and Andy saw each other every other weekend, in San Francisco or in Chicago. At first it had all been fine, Andy had even tried ice once or twice to make love with more vigour and intensity, but now the situation had changed for the worse. Aldo stayed alone in San Francisco and doped himself up every day. Money was beginning to run out and Andy was afraid that Aldo would get into trouble or die, or get even more aggressive and beat him up for real. And worse still, he had read somewhere, in a serious place, a report from the Department of Health or somewhere like that, that once you stopped taking it the depression and lethargy would be so great that your behaviour would deteriorate and it could easily lead to suicide.

The situation turned somewhat tense, Francis talking about the need to retain one's dignity, never to accept aggressive or violent behaviour, physical or verbal, and Andy talking about his hope for Aldo, his determination to accept what was coming so as to be able to spend time at his side. Francis spoke of the contradictions of his behaviour and the need to reflect seriously on this relationship without a future, perhaps even without a present. Andy was crying as they exited the museum and made for East Monroe, where they had left the car outside the Palmer House Hotel, a gem from the Hilton company.

They crossed Clark and took Jackson Boulevard, which led them to the highway for the airport, leaving behind the mythical Sears Tower, which had once held some world record, but whose fame had now been eclipsed by more modern buildings in Singapore, Tokyo or Kuala Lumpur. Talking about architecture made them want to smoke in stochastic association with ideas and relations of improbable causality. They spoke of Francis and Rose's situation, of the changes the relationship had suffered and the expectations and the ex-futures that had flourished after the illness set in.

Andy thought that Rose's strength might snap overnight once Francis had gone from seeing poorly to not seeing anything at all, the absolute zero point of vision, the point where light freezes and gives the retinas no stimulus or the retinas receive the light and cannot process it. They also talked about a mutual friend, Bill O'Malley, a stray dog in that stifling society, a convinced Marxist and a passionate reader of Nelson Algren and Richard Wright,

Ned Rorem and Gore Vidal, as innocent, sometimes, and as enthusiastic as a fish swimming endlessly round a glass bowl.

Once they got to the airport they changed the subject. They spoke a little of Clodio and his development over the last few years. They talked about Rose and her career, which sucked up all her energy. Andy hinted at certain doubts about Rose's future behaviour, but he tried not to dwell on a topic they had already talked about enough, with excessive fears and precautions. They had a little time and so they decided to go outside the main airport building for a cigarette, near the bus stop that brought the guests from the best hotels in Chicago. As they smoked the last Marlboro Light, before Francis boarded for Madrid, they embarked on a conversation that began somewhat awkwardly but gradually thawed as time went on and each of them recovered from the depth charges set off by the other.

"Now that I'm really going, I can tell you something," Francis said sadly. "I came to Chicago with two objectives: to see your body for the last time, before my eyes turn themselves off forever, and to advise you to overhaul your relationship with Aldo. Aldo is going to destroy you, Andy. Please be careful."

"I didn't want it to be the last time," said Andy as softly as he could.

"Me neither. The next time I will be able to tell it is you by ear, from that peachy voice of yours."

"Always so silly. How can a voice be peachy?"

"What questions you ask. Of course it can. It's like silk. And satin. And stone. Voices can have all sorts of textures."

"You're starting to talk as if your sight really was going."

"It is," Francis said and, as he said it, he put on the glasses that served to protect his eyes, and which helped him to see a little, only a little, better.

"I didn't know..."

"I didn't want you to see me this way..."

"That's nonsense. I've been wearing glasses since I was seven. Lots of folks wear glasses and so what. I don't know where this ridiculous complex has come from."

"Soon enough I'll stop wearing them. There'll be no retinas to protect."

"Stop talking that way, you're depressing me."

"Now that I see you better I cannot explain to myself how I could have left you, how I could have allowed you to leave my side over a foolish matter."

"We always want what we don't have. You and I are exactly alike in that. You made a change and I changed a partner. In the end, neither of us was satisfied and neither of us knows, really, why we did it. Don't worry. Nobody's to blame, and nobody wins, no victims or losers."

"I should have said it. I should have confessed I still love you and I couldn't. It hurt! I'm a fool. An almost-blind, wandering fool."

"Don't beat yourself up. Coming to talk to me is the best thing you could have done. I don't know what to think about what you've said but I'll think it over carefully, I promise. You're right when you say my thing with Aldo can't go on like this."

They were on their way into the international-departures hall when the loudspeakers announced the departure of the American Airlines flight to Madrid. Andy stuck as close as he could to Francis. They embraced. They embraced even more closely than when, hours before, they had seen each other again in the airport. A sixth sense or a review of the facts and circumstances, of what they had said and not said, brought them to the same conclusion: it was the last time they would be able to look into each other's faces and recognize each other. A new phase was beginning for both of them, a terrible destiny or unforeseeable conclusion. They were both blubbing, like orphaned children or innocents before the scaffold. It was, definitively, the last time they embraced, caressed each other's necks, kissed passionately to the surprise of the people hurrying through the corridors and halls of O'Hare airport.

Elis Regina wasn't there to sing *Nada será como antes*, nor was Frank Sinatra, rather more American and more from Chicago, to sing *I've Got You Under My Skin*, and they – both of them – missed Elis and Frank.

12

His nephew Clodio had space in his house. As well as space and a good nature, he had plenty of holidays and time to receive and take care of his uncle Francis, the adventurer and exile, the most recent emigrant in a family of emigrants, who had travelled the American continent from New York to Puerto Montt, from Cali to São Paulo, from Matanzas to Baja California. Galicians condemned to emigration, in the past and present, the continuum of a branded family, a rebel family, men forged in liberty who cannot live in a captive, humiliated nation, its existence denied a thousand times over by señoritos brought up in indignity and by the broods of angry young men reared in the worst possible kind of rain, that of the negation of identity, the negation of themselves, as a people and as a race.

For months, the airports had been in chaos. The pilots had scheduled a work-to-rule strike, nobody really knew why. Methods can betray a just cause and the end doesn't always justify the means (there are no archangelic ends at any price: they don't exist). And, because of the strike, there was a kind of international alert, so that when they told Francis that his connection in Madrid might be delayed by seven hours or seventeen, twenty minutes or a whole day, he called Clodio and they agreed to meet at Padrón train station. Francis would let Clodio know when he landed at Santiago and he would take the first train for Padrón. Three or four kilometres from there and they would be at the house, where at different times in their lives the two had played as children alongside the bamboo that played Aeolian percussion concertos when the wind was high, beneath the hundred-year-old *hórreo*, the granary where they stored the wood for the hearth and grates, the enormous, thorn-covered agave trees, the cherry trees in the garden whose lower branches they climbed to gnaw on the cherries until they got indigestion, the trunk of the magnificent apple tree where mushrooms grew every year, but which produced apples like grains of sand, with amazing prodigiousness.

At first there was a sense of distance and froideur. Francis went to kiss his nephew in an unfortunate greeting, a gesture that is fine in the cosmopolitan city but in bad taste elsewhere. The froideur, the surprise, the icy surface of Clodio's hand on Francis's chest stopping his approach, lasted longer than either of them wanted until they left the station car park and an angel passed over to tell them not to go on like that a moment longer, and, of course, the jokes and laughter began, the reminiscences about Clodio's last visit to California, and the plans for both the immediate future (tactics) and a more long-range future (strategy).

Family news hadn't been good in recent months. Their great-grandmother had died, at a great age and with ivy curling around her hips and throat, nineteen births and fifteen adult children, originally from Muros, with the gaze of a Celtic Penelope, weaving and reweaving scarves as she awaited the sons who had emigrated, the daughters who had left to follow their husbands, the grandchildren who never came back because everything went wrong for them – a cursed family – awaiting, until the end, a happiness permanently denied, a long-postponed reunion, even the least bit of satisfaction for her peace of mind. Their great-grandmother had died, she who, against all laws of nature had survived all her offspring scattered throughout the tropics and regions of the south, throughout the American megalopolises and the villages of the Andean mountains. Emigration had devoured them all with its terrible claws. After a few years of frequent contact, the letters became ever sparser until they no longer came at all. In time, also in dribs and drabs, news came of deaths, one by one, terrible in their scanty communications, laconic, brutal, unthinkable in other latitudes and other less raw and cold cultures.

Clodio had brought his little Japanese car, which in his opinion was a good little runner, although an insidious, muted noise, a hum or a rattle, betrayed certain deficiencies in its running. From the station, they followed the road north to the cemetery at Adina, at the foot of the church of Santa María de Iria Flavia, where they had laid Great-Grandmother to rest.

The cemetery was small and not very well cared for, a consequence of the indolence of the families of the dead and the Church's lack of interest in taking care of its heritage.

Nobody from the family had appeared at Great-Grandmother's funeral, at the house or at the cemetery. Clodio had ended up with the finca, not as an inheritance, because there was no will, but in the absence of any other relative who might have a claim on the property. If one of the American family showed up to claim something, they would try to negotiate a solution, but for the time being he would look after the house. "In any case," he said to Francis, "you know you can use it whenever you like. There are plenty of rooms and lots of space in the orchard. What we can't do is sell it, neither of us, until the official period has elapsed. We'll have to make a declaration of interest and it all takes time. Lots of time."

Clodio worked in Santiago, in a publisher's warehouse, but now, since the beginning of the holiday his bosses had allowed him to take early to coincide with Francis's arrival, he was spending every night at the house in the village, more comfortable and spacious than the flat in Santiago, which he was already thinking about selling.

Great-Grandmother Maria was said to have been a woman of strong character. Her entire life story, nonetheless, could be summarized as bringing nineteen children into the world, after her marriage, in the port of Muros, at the tender age of sixteen, to a Civil Guard, one of the nineteenth-century ones, who had not yet perpetrated a systematic betrayal of the rights and dignity of their fellow men, one of those who patrolled the countryside, pausing at every tavern, at every crossroads, at every junction, at every churchyard. In that woman, gracious and violent, conservative and rebellious, affectionate and pitiless, authoritarian and cordial – at once dove and serpent – the essence of the matriarchal line, the saga of the García family, who had sweated blood across the Americas and suffered hunger and persecution in an inhospitable and ungrateful country that submits its children to the shame of not knowing if they will return to rest in their homeland, all came to an end. This had been her entire life story, giving up children to emigration and children who gave children up to emigration, and despite it all there she was, alive in Francis and Clodio's memory, appearing there in her wide-brimmed headscarf, her ebony walking stick, black of clothes and heart, with the appearance of a fleshy, ageing Barbara Stanwyck, giving orders to right and left while people ran their asses off to obey. Now no longer, now forever absent, their gracious great-grandmother, a woman and a half, breeder of a family of exiles.

They soon left the cemetery, bounded by its wall and a hedge of myrtle, spotted with the odd olive tree – more common in those latitudes than the stereotype, based on differentiation and exclusion, would have it – after taking a few minutes to pray or murmur their coded messages to the dead woman, for whom, in truth, whether from unfamiliarity or negative personal experience, neither of the two had much affection.

On the way they passed the Trulock house, which belonged to the family descended from John Trulock, an English engineer who, in the last quarter of the nineteenth century, had designed the railway between Santiago de Compostela and Carril, in the province of

Pontevedra, near Vilagarcía de Arousa and facing the island of Cortegada. Jorge Trulock – Don Jorgito, as the locals called him, for his slight stature and sickly countenance – had been Francis's first English teacher, when Francis still spent summers with his parents at Porta dos Mariños and took his bicycle every day to cycle the two kilometres between his house and the Trulock place. Francis had very fond memories of him, of Don Jorgito, his methods and his patience, his exquisite manners and the affection he showed him. Don Jorgito had died fifteen years earlier, during a very hot summer when a terrible fire had destroyed part of the house. The fire had started upstairs, because of a portable stove that had fallen on to some curtains, and, in an old house like that, it had spread rapidly. When the flames reached the roof and, responding to his wife's pleas, Don Jorgito went back into the house in search of a pet dog that had been trapped upstairs. Despairing of the fate that might have befallen the dog and displaying a cross-species altruism characteristic of people with great affection for those unlike them, Don Jorgito ran in to look for it and met, poor man, the same fate as the dog. Unjust and terrible.

They continued along the local road towards Pousa, passing the sugar plant and the lamp factory. Both still sad from their reminiscences, Clodio brought Francis up to date on the most recent events to have overshadowed village life. The widening of a road that passed through their village – Pazos – had endangered the peaceful coexistence of the locals. An eccentric route, owing more to the vindictive wrath of an unpleasant local mayor than a qualified engineer, had completely disrupted the equilibrium of the village without bringing a single benefit for its inhabitants. And this hadn't been the worst thing; the works had begun precisely with their family's home, their family who had been particularly involved in the resistance to that useless work, proposing an alternative route. The result had been catastrophic, dozens of properties razed by the machines, families in conflict, insults like gravestones, enthusiastic and unjust acts by the (in)security forces, indifferent politicians (of all parties and creeds, without exception) and, to top it all, an unfinished project and many properties destroyed by subsidence and the idiocy of a gang of ignorant fools. Clodio's veins swelled as he talked about it, as he remembered each episode and each action, each desertion of friends or neighbours, each tardy response from the politicians (all of them, of all parties and creeds without exception, whether sitting on the right or left of Our Father). Clodio's temples were about to explode from sheer rage when they reached Porta dos Mariños, their family seat and longed-for port of arrival and protection from the storm.

The bulldozers and mechanical diggers had destroyed the overhead vine that separated the front door from the road, cut off half the drive where they usually parked the family cars and swept before them, with a complete lack of respect, a fantastical path of myrtle bushes and a few orange trees. And all this for nothing, destruction for the sake of it, with no intention of using the land they had razed, just for the pleasure of destroying the properties of a few families who had not gone along with the client-based system of the party currently in power and who, it seemed, also lacked the seal of authenticity and popular support to be represented by those who weren't in power. Shameful. The law of the strongest as the only natural law, the inevitable ruin of a land of dwarves.

Round the back almost everything was still the same, the ancient bamboo that flourished in the spring, the abundant apple trees that brought the summer to an end with a profusion of fruit, the *hórreo* that sheltered the firewood in the autumn and the secrets of the harvest and the cellar with its family gatherings for moving the barrels and for making firewater when winter was at its coldest. The only thing obviously and traumatically lacking, beyond the destructive raid carried out at the side of the road, was the fig tree, an immense fig tree that produced magnificent fruit twice a year.

"And what happened to the fig tree?" asked Francis, surprised.

"Hurricane Hortense took the fig tree. A long while back. I was still on the cod-fishing boats. Don't you remember, that sort of hurricane that flattened half the country? It crossed Newfoundland, where I was on the *Uralde*, the boat that later went down during an Atlantic crossing. Then it crossed the Atlantic, all the way to the Galician coast. We heard about it at sea. On the radio. It was devastation. Then we got hit by Klaus – they had started by then to give the hurricanes men's names, the feminists, you know, always focusing on the important things – and it gave us a beating that still makes the hairs on my chest stand on end just thinking about it."

"That Hortense must have been quite something to carry off the fig tree," Francis noted as Clodio accompanied him inside the house, carrying his suitcase and looking out something to drink, to celebrate their reunion.

Francis was thrilled to sleep in the same room as on his previous visit, a dozen years earlier. It was a large room, with a high ceiling and a wooden floor, an uncomfortable iron bed with peeling paint, a chest full of photo albums – testament and memory of the Indies – and some never-worn christening robes that had acquired a tinge somewhere between milky coffee and the yellow of damp and Barolo wine, and a window that looked out on to an espalier where various fruit trees were growing, including a tree of mandarin oranges that brought Francis many memories and a great deal of nostalgia.

As soon as they entered the room, Clodio, who had helped carry his case, took his leave. He was going to call Luisa to tell her that Francis had arrived and that he would expect her for dinner tomorrow.

Shortly afterwards Clodio came to call for his uncle Francis, who was unpacking his suitcase and arranging his clothes in the wardrobe.

"Come on, Uncle, let's give ourselves something to celebrate."

They went down to the cellar and broke into a barrel of red wine, as one does in these reunions, when many years or experiences have gone by. Clodio and Francis spoke of their past friendship, of how despite the age difference, family status and tendencies – eight years, different generation and a few ounces of ambiguity in Francis's favour – for five years they had shared parties and pilgrimages, celebrations and concerts all over the Ulla area. Francis told him about his break-up with Andy and how he had fallen in love with Rose, so quickly and intensely.

Clodio, for his part, spoke of his relationship with Luisa, how he had met her when he had just come back off the boat and she was still at university. At first he hadn't known what to do, whether to tell her about his youthful adventures or say nothing. They had been going out for some time when he told her everything about his past. She was very understanding, and said they were the normal adolescent doubts, when one still doesn't know one's own feelings. She didn't think it was important. He, for his part, once the moments of doubt had passed, had adopted the easiest position, as he said with a melancholy expression somewhere between resignation and nostalgia.

The hours ticked by in talking and drinking, remembering anecdotes and picking over their lives and other people's. After the first few glasses they fell into a nostalgic daze, which plunged them into the worst of themselves. Both had tried to celebrate the reunion calmly, letting feelings return to their place, risking little in their movements, with self-control and a steady pulse. Tomorrow would be another day and, after some rest and reflection, everything would appear in a new light. They both thought this, at the same time, like skilled diviners.

They had spoken of many things, of the past and the present, how they would manage life in the house, of Luisa and Rose – the women in their lives – of projects and future plans. But they had not spoken of blindness.

13

He had originally considered taking advantage of his trip
across the Atlantic to interview the Portuguese writer,
Saramago, that sturdy fellow with the face of a tortoise
whose chelonian back probably held coded messages for
understanding his novels, for threshing out every inch
of symbolism in the parables he told, the situations he
described with such precision and detail. After a while he
had changed his mind. What would the author of *Ensaio
sobre a Cegueira* say if an almost-blind man came to
see him, a translator who had lost his sight in the middle
of translating this very novel? Would he feel (even
grudgingly) responsible or terribly indifferent? Would
he feel remorse or enjoy the paradox? It didn't matter. He
wouldn't go and see him. At least not for the moment. He
was a long way behind on the project. He couldn't turn
up at the author's house with all his doubts and queries,
with half a novel still to translate – he had a first draft,
but that wasn't enough for a serious interview – and
with no clear idea of what to ask and how. Having to
subject his short-term projects to such a huge volley of

worries sapped his energy and, furthermore, dear old Saramago lived in seclusion on Lanzarote, one of the Canary Islands, which couldn't be reached directly from Santiago (or maybe it could, but to justify his decision, he had decided not to consult any travel agents). Aeroplanes had to be taken when there was no alternative, but they weren't his favourite thing. So he decided that perhaps it would be better to make his first approach by letter, to introduce himself and sketch out a few specific questions about the first part of the novel. By the time he received a response, he would be a lot further along with the project and would be able to be more specific with his questions. This would mean upping the tempo of his work. Francis always liked working under pressure, but under pressure of his own making, with a few medium-term deadlines made to be broken and a final submission date which he always reached *in extremis*, with two or three sleepless nights or a few marathon, sixteen-hour sessions and plenty of coffee, obsessive and rather unhealthy periods of reclusion and isolation and plenty of coffee, ignoring the phone and wandering the house like a zombie, in pyjamas and slippers, three days' worth of stubble and rumpled hair, looking a complete fright.

As he did whenever he reviewed the progress of the project, he spent several hours in intense concentration, working out a timetable and measuring out the deadlines, noting down short-term objectives and sketching out scenarios for various possible events, setting aside very specific slots for friends and leisure, and marking out the time as if he was working on a symphony. Afterwards he might or might not follow the plans – more likely not, or at least not completely – but the planning helped him to steer clear of despair or a panicked fall into the void, helped him to imagine himself moving forward with the project and working at variable speed through the stages. Then there were always surprises – phone calls that disturbed the peace, friends who showed up unannounced, minor domestic catastrophes – which slowed progress and rebalanced priorities, but they were familiar pressures and sloughs, part of his work and life, the scalar component of his way of being.

One of his reasons for coming to Galicia had been specifically to avoid interruptions, but he hadn't counted on the greatest interruption, the one he couldn't avoid, the one he couldn't escape: himself. The idea of blindness, of absolute darkness, and the slow but constant advancement of the illness had plunged him into a reactive depression, a classic – and understandable – consequence of feeling or experiencing misfortune. The depression regularly brought him to the point of inertia, something he now had to avoid, to rise above in any way he could. During his last few days in California he had tried taking refuge in the miracle pill, Prozac – what they called the happy pill – and now after a few weeks he was starting to see the first, albeit not definitive, results. He wanted to live and work, which was something. What he didn't want was to go blind, to have to limit his activity, to lose his footing in the familiar world.

Every morning he walked in the woods or through the fields by the river, to shake out his spirit and to think. The flow of the water with its harmonious, eternal sound, gave him a strange feeling of relaxation. Thinking about Rose and about work. About Andy and his problems. About blindness and ways of keeping hope alive and not falling into despair. The pills helped, but it wasn't only them, he had to do the rest, every morning, every day, at every moment. To avoid plunging into the pooling blackness. To maintain his dignity. To survive.

Zoe was always willing to go out, to go for a walk behind the house, towards the woods and the rabbits, or to wander towards the banks of the Sar as it crosses the plain, so fertile thanks to the annual floods and so uncultivated. That morning, as soon as Francis had put on his wellingtons to go out for his morning walk, Zoe was ready to accompany him with the interested devotion of a well-trained bitch who wasn't too fussy about the company she kept. Zoe wanted to go out for a walk. It started raining and Francis decided that going out walking might not be the greatest idea. Sometimes we make decisions for the benefit of others, and this is even truer when it comes to animals. When they have to piss, when it's time to eat, when they can go for a walk and when they can't, and, in the end, whether or not they will be given a lethal injection (poor thing, so she doesn't suffer).

Once the rain had stopped – a torrent as intense as it was brief – he went out with Zoe towards the woods, along the hollow way that runs towards Pedroso do Vendaval, a minuscule village clinging to a hill surrounded by the absurd mishmash of oak and eucalyptus so typical of Galicia. He was planning to make for a beautiful piece of marshland where as a boy he had been told that very early in the morning, almost at dawn, the Nereids appeared; it bordered an oak and laurel woodland to the south and, to the north, the stream that comes down from the Agro do Cínico, its thundering clear waters winding their way down between willow trees, brambles, elm groves and alders. Francis and Zoe said goodbye to Clodio, who stayed behind in the orchard digging over the ground and putting down horse manure, so – now that they were coming to the end of spring – he could sow beans and onions, lettuces and peas, peppers and tomatoes.

As they walked, images of the past came into his mind, ideas, recurring obsessions accompanied by an itching feeling, from the nettles or the thistles that lined the paths. Going back to the village, for Francis, was something of an exploration of roots, a modern epic (Clodio transformed, overnight, into a self-sufficient, wholegrain farmer, a recycled urbanite, who had a dog with the name of a goddess or a test-tube baby, a cheerful entomologist girlfriend, a nourishing job and a renewed passion for pirate stories), an epic story of flight into the future (the delayed crisis of not being what one wants to be), of essential reflection (values, reference points, lost youth, change of state), of ritual ceremony (perpetuation of friendship, tolerance, loyalty), of romantic discovery, of umbilical refuge and welcoming fields.

Francis and Clodio, despite (or, perhaps, because of) the age difference, had maintained a close platonic relationship when they were both much younger. Clodio greatly admired his uncle Francis, so strong and so intelligent, and Francis was happy in the company of his nephew, so beloved, so vital and with so much energy. It had never gone beyond a friendship based on mutual protection and affection, but when they had been separated for a long time – the first time Francis left to work in the US – each had felt the other's absence, although a needless reticence meant it took them some time to admit it. The passage of time, which modifies our scale of values, and successive encounters with people (men and women) who had influenced their lives, decanted the sediment of that tendency and generated a sexual identity characterized by few certainties and many, many doubts.

The walk was short. Although it was the beginning of June, rain was a frequent occurrence in the area. So frequent that, during his first week there, Francis couldn't recall going out walking once without the protection and shelter of an umbrella. Zoe had tired quickly or perhaps sensed the rain through a sixth sense, like a meteorological Argos watching over her master. She half turned and refused to go on along the lane that led down to the marshes. Francis had no choice but to turn back towards the house. When they reached the shed, a short, intense rain shower began, with bubbling puddles, its duration unforeseeable. It caught them going through the gate to the orchard, just by the bamboo. Without really knowing why, they paused beneath the overhead vine, watching the water falling with the violence of an unleashed force. Francis felt as if he had been there before, many times, as a child. Only one thing was missing. The fig tree. OK, two things. The fig tree and the view, which was diminishing so fast he now couldn't see beyond the bamboo border. Suddenly he felt a shiver down his spine. Dreams. What must the dreams of the blind be like?

Just then, Francis took a photograph of Rose from his pocket, the one they had taken on the shores of Lake Michigan, with Andy and Aldo. Two couples trying to survive a great snowstorm – when the thermometer had plummeted to thirty-two below zero on the centigrade scale, which wasn't the one they used on the weather reports, but the one they understood better – when, without really knowing why, they realized they were two potentially exchangeable couples, that Francis still liked Andy and vice versa, that Aldo and Rose, a liberal Irishwoman and a stimulant-addicted Chicano, made a fine pair, that Rose and Andy talked about music and computers, local politics and trips to Europe, while Aldo and Francis had more in common than their love for Andy and talked of literature and Marxism, thrillers and Latin music. Rose was far away, but Rose had learned to walk on the beach gazing at the horizon, analyzing the remains of shipwrecks, waiting out an infinite vigil for a nomadic Ulysses who didn't know how to plan his return, who contrary to the spirit of the original legend had let himself be seduced by the silence of the mermaids, had become a slave of the Cyclopes and had lost his bearings on his voyage home (poor Ulysses with no recognizable Ithaca and no compass, no ship and no memory). Francis thought Rose should have come over by now, Rose, a weaving Penelope.

It took time for the sky to clear, as it always does when the drops make bubbles in the puddles. Clodio had gone out to run some errands and left a note saying he would be back late – "after twelve," the note said, "don't expect me for dinner" – and warning him not to let Zoe in the house. The moon came out to take a turn along the Milky Way, which was visible even though it wasn't a Holy Year, or a mimetic and mediocre celebration of the Camino de Santiago. Zoe was howling outside, unable to understand why Francis wouldn't let her in (orders from her master who had left a vague but categorical note, who is out somewhere, letting himself be loved at some soirée). Francis wasn't howling, although he had listened to Cyril Collard singing *Paradise*, from the soundtrack of *Les Nuits Fauves*. Now, after the third or fourth song, Francis wondered whether Zoe wasn't howling precisely to make him change the music, when René-Marc Bini was warbling *Lifeline (I believe in your lifeline because you could be an angel too)*. Too much. He couldn't bear so much concentrated foolishness on a single CD, so he got up from the chair and put on something by Nyman, which had the therapeutic effect of a balsam.

Zoe, grateful, stopped howling. Francis, grateful to Zoe and pleased with his own choice, relaxed his tired expression and read, placidly, from a book by Lezama, "*al borde mismo de la noche extendida de una boca a otra boca.*" He dozed for a while – Nyman or Lezama, or maybe both of them, helped out there – switching in movements as fleeting as they were uncontrollable between waking and sleeping. He had recurring nightmares or ideas. He awoke a little sadder and a little blinder; perceptibly sadder and perceptibly blinder.

Like a premonition – like a magical symbol, a circle within another circle that contains it or complements it in its spherical obsession – night entered disrespectfully into the handful of houses that made up the village of

Pazos. Somebody walked along the road that borders the house and Zoe, who should have barked, had stopped barking at the very edge of night, which crept through the house like Chinese whispers, which was already spreading over the thatched roof and the alabaster bust above the hearth, over the upended bunch of dried roses, over the chicory growing in the cellar, in the darkness of rotted air, of cold, isolated underground. Night falls and everything disappears into the road that borders the house, crocuses and fig trees, agaves and passion flowers, cacti and cypresses, which surround the space, hinting at nature's possibilities and at greatness in the path of evolutionary continuity.

Clodio had gone to visit the stables he kept in an old house along the lane to the meadow, to feed the horses – the mare is pregnant and so she might be giving birth, a night of waiting, a new life budding – and to speak with some neighbours about who knows what, something to do with rights of use over a piece of irrigated land. Francis had stayed behind, alone with the regular ticking of the clock on the wall, accompanied by the odd crow from the spotted cockerel, who had lost control of his circadian rhythms, and by Zoe's sad monologues from the garden (are there monologues that aren't sad? Do gardens particularly invite monologues? Is that why Japanese gardens have little waterfalls and streams? Dogs… can dogs perform monologues?). In any case, better to let Zoe in, it's pouring with rain and the poor thing could catch cold or worse.

The silence was like a balsam, if somehow one can speak of this salve that envelopes everything and gives what the city refuses, what Francis refuses when, every so often, he goes out in search of noise (the bus, the bars, the streets swollen with people heading for unknown destinations, going shopping, for a walk, dragging the filthy depths of other people's glances, attempting to share rites or miseries, swapping chains of conversation or sources of rage).

Francis wanted to believe (it was a process of will) that the city wasn't bad in itself, and he thought about the services, about the theatre and the cinema, about public transport and lectures, retrospective exhibitions and art galleries, about meeting places, and about everything that is true as long as you believe in it like dogma (was the martyrdom of St Tarsicius necessary or a cruel predecessor of the bloodiest horror movies? Was the miracle at the wedding at Cana a commercial move? What romantic relationship united the boys Justus and Pastor so closely? Is St Sebastian's homosexuality dogma? Where is the limbo of the just in the new catechism? What became of those children damned for original sin? and so on, doubting, until the end, or rather until the arrival of the green horse carrying one of the horsemen of the Apocalypse), everything that presents more than just a cause for hesitation, as long as we give the brain time and calcium to relax it a bit and prevent it drowning in the semiotic mirage of the city (the traffic light that takes so long to go green, the yellow sign that indicates the bus stop, the clock that tells the temperature, doors that close indicating the end of the working day, flashing orange lights and ambulances, police officers bundled up like samurais in search of a confrontation, alarms in car showrooms, lines painted on the floor that tell us when we can cross from one pedestrian island to another pedestrian island (God, who could have come up with such a name!), a neon advert for a sex show, loudspeakers announcing a circus or a sale, local elections or sponsored rock concerts, blue posters that indicate an underground train, areas for dogs to defecate in, graffiti tags, trees with blackened leaves and aborted fruit, rubbish, mud, people talking to themselves and chasing ghosts, rounding up the beardless, massacring pigeons with onyx knives, searching for a way out of the labyrinths – one's own or other peoples'…).

That night, Clodio got back quite late. He had already called to say he would be back after midnight. Francis had roasted a rabbit in the oven, delicious, with its sauce of white wine and rosemary, parsley and liver, pounded in the mortar with tender garlic and a little oil flavoured with thyme. When Clodio opened the door and smelled that smell, he quickly gave into his half-drunkenness and gazed at his uncle Francis with the devotion of a lover.

A miniscule incident – Clodio not taking off his shoes on entering the kitchen of an out-of-control and distracted Francis – illustrated the difficulty of coexistence, of respect for established norms, of harmony when two cultures and two ways of being coincide in an enclosed space. In such cases the solution is difficult and negotiation about stopping or starting routines can become problematic. All too often, both sides are guilty of practising one-sided, ill-founded, impulsive or fleeting philosophies.

The contrast between the two situations illustrates the difficulty of coexistence, to be overcome only with a strong dose of respect.

"Uncle Francis, I have told you a thousand and one times not to let the dog in with muddy feet. Look what a mess."

"I'm sorry, Clodio. It was pouring with rain and I thought Zoe would be better off inside. I tried to stop her and wipe her feet, but she got away and came into the kitchen. Nothing I could do. I followed her and walked through the mud from her paws. I was going to clean it up, but I didn't get round to it."

"It's OK, but in future be more careful. Now I've got to clean up and you know how much I like doing that."

Francis thought that living alone is hard work until you get used to the silence, the freedom to break it and the absence of somebody to talk to (some people turn to a pet to alleviate the situation). Monologues help to compensate for other absences and sex is relegated, definitively, to a lesser position. Living – even just for a few days – with somebody who has lived alone for a long time is little short of impossible. Order, implicit norms, rites, perfectly-marked-out territories, are concealed in a flood of codes and principles that make the visit complex and difficult for the newly-arrived visitor.

Clodio was a good sort. After a long journey around Brazil he had come back changed. He had set himself the task of returning to his origins, listening again to the murmur of the grass growing beneath his feet, feeding rabbits and chickens, going out horse riding, making conserves and liqueurs, enjoying silence and walks. Clodio playing his double role of false coenobite and subject of another scale of relation, that of the place where he was born and raised, where he played as a child, where he learned his first letters and the perfume of his first love.

Zoe was now sitting next to Francis, after spending ten minutes winding around his legs. It must be hard to be a pet. Accepting a total loss of freedom in exchange for a bowl of food, when there is one. It must be hard to be a pet, always dependent on your master's passing whims, always having to entertain him in exchange for the right to a bit of food and respect. Being a pet is like being a slave, a chattel to be exchanged along with your whole family, having to be loyal, and completely faithful, and even affectionate and understanding, to a master who isn't always good.

Clodio had come home exhausted and, after looking at the rabbit and exchanging a few words with his uncle Francis, he thought it was time for bed. Tomorrow Luisa would come to spend her holidays in the countryside and he would have to play the host properly.

14

There are different kinds of deaths. Some pay no heed to our need for a swift journey to an illusory better world. Others are certainly a journey, albeit neither swift nor to a better place, but rather an unhurried passage into doubt or oblivion. That kind is a death foretold, like so many others in reality or fiction. Not a total death, with dismemberment and rigor mortis, or even a mental death from Alzheimer's, so familiar, with its disorder in the circuits of memory. No. That kind is a partial death, like an amputated limb and a cold calculation, an aborted reference system, the negation of knowledge structured in shapes and colours, in silhouettes and reliefs, in perspectives and compositions of light, in the casting and creeping of shadows. A death marked out in sensations and measurements. Francis had spent two weeks in the land of his people – who were his people? – the land of learning and Cartesian references, two weeks losing his sight and working on a draft of *Ensaio sobre a Cegueira*, two weeks of bidding a progressive farewell to exterior landscapes – so marvellous in their essence – of fevered dedication to understanding blindness, of visiting it both intellectually and physically.

The phone rang and it was Rose, magnificently witty and overflowing with contagious optimism, flattering him with exaggerated sweet talk, her unrestrained laughter making her seem almost present. Rose talking, announcing her arrival. Rose close by despite the distance, gabbling away about her friends in San Diego and how far along her current project is, how sunny it is in California, and how happy she is at work, all at once in a jumble, a diarrhoea of neural circuits. Rose asking after Francis and Clodio, Luisa and the progress of the translation. Rose talking about Martin's demands – as insistent and tenacious as a rutting stag beetle – and those of the usual friends, who were worrying about Francis and the advance of his blindness. Rose with news of Huo and Lucretius and everyone else. Rose bubbling over and longing to kiss him down the telephone.

"I'm arriving next Monday, eight days from today, on the 11.30 flight from Barcelona."

"We'll be at the airport. I'll sort everything out here. I can't wait to see you."

"Me neither, sweetheart."

"See you soon. Call as soon as you get to Barcelona in case there's a change of some sort. You know… airports… delays…"

"OK, you hang up. See you soon."

"A kiss."

"Right back at you."

Rose's voice vanished into the telephone. Francis missed her. A lot. Rose, sustaining the difficult balance of the couple. Rose, always giving encouragement and congratulations. Rose, dreaming of a future different from the real one, the terrible, imperfect one. Francis longed for her presence, her lavender scent and her talcum-powdered breasts, the immense tenderness of this warm, contradictory female.

The days went by, days that sketch out the borders around the territory of the self, deposit a sediment of ideas and feelings, routine acts and rites to install us in the world. The eight days passed for Francis in the accidental flight of a butterfly flitting from one flower to another, from a bitter feeling to a sweet reflection, from a salty sensation – of tears trickling down cheeks – to the bitter awakening of lungs massacred by cigarette smoke. The eight-day countdown went by in a sob, an impulse, the constant obsession with halting the disease's advance, feigning an unreal state of mind, taking care of himself ready for Rose's arrival, for when they would touch each other again, with that mixture of nostalgia and comfort that touch alone can bring to the lives and dreams of the blind.

At night, after dinner, the house turned into an agora. Clodio and Luisa's friends came over to weave conversations and build dreams, to talk of everything that came into their heads, of eels and comets, the poetry of Rilke or their distaste for politicians and their excesses. The background to these conversations was the house overseen by Clodio, agreeable and different, ruined and rebuilt, desolate and cold, a privileged place for talking until dawn, enveloped in the bluish smoke of the herb that makes you giggle. They talked of philosophy and literature, of music and politics, and who knows what else during those nights of advances and surprises, fondnesses and friendships, mermaids and canticles.

They had come home from the airport, from collecting Rose, who had arrived from America on a flight from Barcelona, but really from San Francisco. Luisa had dropped them at the door and gone to park the car. They had come home and now the hallway was illuminated by a night of rain and storm. First the introductions and then a tour, as hurried and routine as it was impressive, around the vastness of rooms and attics, the columns and mezzanines, the zinc bathtubs and tropical wood banisters and then, for a change of scene, to the welcoming snug, home to fraying armchairs, whisky and leisurely conversation. They talked of the chemical reaction that produces the glow-worm's light and Luisa's entomological travels, of nearly-blind animals and fights between male stag beetles, which Luisa, with the patience of a biblical character, had recorded on a videotape they now lingered over, as it moderated their joy, kept the nervousness of the reunion at bay, diverted their attention from the forbidden topics of which it was better not to speak. It wasn't easy to know how they had come to be talking of environmental protestors, but they were, had been, and would be still when the morning star announced the arrival of the day at that cold hour just before dawn. Nothing in particular had happened – dinner, conversation, drinks, glow-worms, a bit of gentle music to waft them along on the smoke of dreams, the stag beetles and their ritual fights, the environmentalists, some cinema and a few drops of jazz – but it had been a singular night, the kind of night when those present believe they have just awoken from an obsessive dream that has gone on too long, the kind of night that marks a before and after, fuses solidarities and germinates new coordinates. A unique, fantastic, unrepeatable night.

The days were gone that marked out territories, calls for help and appeals, tribal behaviours and ancient habits more closely linked to individual routines than to the atavistic determinisms tied to a life sentence. Rose had arrived, bringing positive and negative ions, charged with static electricity and ambivalence of spirit, with impulses hoarded during the weeks of separation, caresses amassed like jewels to be distributed to the masses, floating on a refractive surface. It was her world, almost always happy, but now anguished by the small inconveniences of everyday life and a little paranoid, justifiably submerged in a reactive depression.

Those days were gone and it was better now, with less distance and more comfort, fewer absences and more company, albeit with some restriction of their social circle, the relationship exclusive to an unhealthy extent. Tunnel vision and an immense tunnel in their relationship, monothematic and monorhythmic, monomaniacal and monotonous.

"If you have loved a place, never go back. It only leads to frustration." That was something Ernst Jünger had been told by his father and that he repeated, a centenarian now, but still lucid and with a long memory, giving interviews and speaking a little of everything. Rose was of the same opinion, although she restricted it to holidays, and she never went back to a place, however much she liked it. Francis was a little like that as well, although he didn't take it to such radical extremes. It was Rose's first visit, she had never been to Galicia and everything was new and so similar in some ways to Ireland, her island of mixed feelings, but for Francis it was somehow both a blessing and a curse.

Bad luck meant that one evening Francis felt the temptation to visit some of the haunts of his youth, of his first romantic steps in autumn, muted colours and ferrous deposits. He came upon the meadow beside Chan de Abeleira, a little amphibian paradise with a marshy wetland, surrounded by oak trees, laurels and redwoods. A track, which might well pass through other less epic gorse bushes, dividing what had previously been a humid micro-ecosystem, home of mists and grass snakes, territory and shelter of fauns and frog princes, through a dusty and unusable wound.

Those in power at the moment were the worst kind of idiots, brandishing their ignorance and backwardness like standards, massacring common sense and sharing out the spoils won from a people abandoned to lethargy. Those in power were the kind who did a great deal of ill, who beat their breasts, sharing out what did not belong to them, but was placed in their hands and which they used to warm the bellies of the docile. Perhaps power was always in the hands of the forces of fear and immobility, of reaction against necessary change and against the evolution of the human spirit. They brandished the phantasms of fear and thus won the power that kept them in business, perks and all.

Francis's eyes got wetter, an intense cold shivered down his spine, and suddenly he understood what it was to grow old, what it was to have your heart furrowed with stigmas, what time was, and loneliness, and the immense impotence his elders had felt when a tree was uprooted, when a wall fell down, when a millennial rock bled granite as it became a quarry, when they destroyed a Roman road or submerged a village beneath a reservoir. Life from now on would be different and difficult, no longer being able to take refuge in familiar landscapes, the trails carpeted with leaves of walnut, beech, chestnut or oak trees, along which the torrent of the rainy season descends from the mountain. For the first time, after so many years, of going, of coming, of travelling and returning to the umbilical cord of the family, he felt the shock of return, the sensation that some things had changed in his absence and were no longer there. They no longer exist, they belong exclusively to the world of memories and dreams. Then he understood the fear that returning produced in him, fear of the drying out of his roots and an enormous vacuum. He raised his voice and said, with nobody to hear him, "Let me act like a homecoming traveller. Let me cry, for a while, like a poor boy with a broken heart. Let me feel intensely strong, surrounded by the weakness of tortured nature." Then he remembered a conversation he had had with Rose and exclaimed, "Jünger's father was right!"

Back at home, after a traumatic encounter with the favourite spot from his magical childhood, his mind was filled with flights and returns, the farewells on the quays of Vigo, when his entire family had deserted in search of the American paradise, his own farewell at the airport, when he decided to try his luck on the other side of the pond – nobody called it the pond any more – with the temerity of youth and the impetuous spirit so characteristic of his stock. Ports of arrival and departure, of pulling into quays and loosening moorings, dreams and shipwrecks, voyages and adventures. Ports of arrival and departure, of leaving so you could cease to exist, of arrival at a port safe from mutation and change. Innocence made to be lost. Always a tropism, which follows flight with return, the temptation of paradise with the hangover of return to a familiar hell. An eternal return to the familiar cradle, like homecoming travellers, sobbing like children with broken hearts, feeling themselves strong and renewed, sad but resolved to advance through tortured nature.

Rose had brought his mail, almost all of it junk mail from the banks and catalogue companies, subscription renewals and all that. By chance there was also something more personal, from Katty and Pal, so happy and hippy in their house in Santa Monica, as well as a postcard from Dougal – good old Dougal never forgot his friends – in the forests of Jerangau, in search of the Malaysian tiger, and even – a surprise after so long without news – a letter from Negra, a friend from way back, surely travelling in the southern latitudes of her beloved Buenos Aires, to return to Bilbao, to leave the Madrid of those times of adventure and oceans, *stormy weather*, friends and visits, to return to that old bar where they sold arbutus-berry brandy and beetroot cakes. A letter from Negra, so ethnic and so different, always so rebellious and so smiling, so impregnated with aromas and rhythms, who signed off with this typically Rioplatense paragraph:

Now I'm off to catch a train to carry me through the mists to a little breakwater from which you can glimpse infinity. Lots of love.

A letter from Negra that must be answered soon because he senses her lost in multiple sorrows, travelling to forget, a romantic seeking comfort in the past, caressing his neck with a new voltage, which makes him feel she is there, there is no need to call her or give her more than what she asks: a distant presence, a heartfelt sentence, absent words. A great kiss that echoes on the paper, which gives it back improved and extravagant, perfumed and omnipresent, sensual and Guarani.

Life at home was organized very simply. Francis and Rose spent all day working. Francis wrote and corrected the translation on a portable computer he had bought way back when, to use on journeys and visits. Rose, for her part, and although she was on vacation, spent most of her time working on programming questions, reading technical journals or accompanying Luisa on one of her entomological excursions (to call them excursions was a euphemism, given that they only rarely left the orchard, to seek out an anthill in the nearby pinewoods, or to find a wasps' nest on a rocky ledge, a place on the riverbank to watch the dragonflies or the water boatmen, a fallen tree in the woods from which to extract larvae or the acorns of an oak tree from which to find worms or insect eggs). Clodio, for his part, was kept busy all day, from early in the morning, and Luisa divided her time between the faculty and her fieldwork, collecting photographic images, or recording films about insects, her favourite animals. At night it was different, they all gathered in the kitchen, ate – almost always fish despite Rose's taste and Huo's absence – and told endless anecdotes, talking about projects, music and literature, one topic after another. Nothing was forbidden, although politics and sport, the economy and celebrity gossip rarely entered the mix. They spent their days like this, with the gentle pleasure of vacation, harmony, camaraderie between the couples and satisfying work, each absorbed in their own surroundings until night brought a shared world.

Like every evening, after a sparse dinner of tuna salad and seasonal fruit and a few conversations over the table with Rose and Luisa, Francis carried a chair out beneath the overhead vine, in the central alley, where the basin for washing clothes was, and sat down to correct the proofs of the translation that soon, within a few days, he would have to send to Martin. Before beginning his evening's work, he lit a cigarette, his favourite brand, and took a few puffs to focus his mind on the work and get himself started. He liked it when the agreed deadline was approaching and his work was progressing, particularly in the last few days; he liked feeling there were still things to do and he hadn't yet done enough to feel liberated, to feel that kind of asphyxia that helped him so much in the long evening sessions that so often dragged on into the following dawn. The pressure was unbearable, like a heavy flagstone. On the one hand there was the urgency of the publisher to have the edition in the shops before the Swedish Academy made its decision, and, on the other, his own personal urgency with his inevitably fading eyes, which had already lost precise focus and depth of field, were already just imperfect instruments, defective, in need of special lenses. A lot of pressure and a lot of doubts, like Theseus in the labyrinth, face to face with the Minotaur without the help of one of Ariadne's threads to hang on to.

A butterfly flitted by, pausing to suck in the bowl of the lips of a flower. The water in the washbasin – transparent and lucid, pristine and encircled by the stones – seemed a coralline depth, from a tropic that was physically distant and yet so close in this orchard of emigrants and bamboos. The wind bent the willows to the limits of their elasticity. He didn't know why he thought of Deng, the little Maoist mandarin, with his collarless jacket and the desiccation of a prostatic old man, with the wily gaze of a surviving bureaucrat. The butterfly fluttered off, Francis thought automatically of the coldness of the summary executions, the wounded dragon with bloody, broken claws and fetid breath, hurling out fire through its enormous nostrils. These were spurious, largely meaningless associations, only related very tangentially, a kind of hallucination at the height of the vigil, in the very middle of the work, a consequence of his fear of losing images, of feeling the geometry of the vacuum, of marking out specific fields and territories.

Francis never found out what Newton felt during the event with the siesta and the apple. Now, sitting beneath the overhead vine, hearing the burbling of the water in the pipes of the basin, watching for butterflies fluttering in random directions, making curls, scales and corkscrews, he awaited the ancient apple tree that would illuminate him, would help him stop the world to find his place, to feel he had strength, to continue fighting the advancing confusion, the advancing blindness. Innocence made to be lost, to vanish when destiny marks a crossroads, when the reality that confronts itself is marked by irreversible fate, like Newton's apple, like the summary executions, like blindness. This was being an adult, he thought, knowing your limits, marking out territories with the fluids from your sphincter, saying this is as far as I go and I can't go any further, closing doors and opening gates, discovering that freedom has obstacles and contretemps, choices at the crossroads, projections that, while possible, always exist. That was life, conformity, the easy renunciation of projects, desires, ambitions to change the world.

Sitting in his wicker chair, Francis let the pages fall on to the flagstone beside him, lit another cigarette, lowered his eyelids and rested with his eyes closed. Meanwhile, the water flowed from the green pipe into the basin – water upon water, force upon force, lapping the flagstones where nobody washed clothes any longer – bringing his mind a sense of harmonious equilibrium. Just then – a fantasy of sleeplessness, a hallucination, perhaps – he remembered a day like this, in that same place and probably July because it was very hot with few clouds and little wind. He was playing in the basin, which was still sometimes used for washing, making battles with boats and somebody was washing clothes on the enormous stone, somebody who jumped in surprise at the cries coming from the shed, a female voice, Electra screaming at the top of her lungs, the ancestral lament of an athletic wailer. Somebody had died in Cuba. He realized it by the stink of that wail that mixed misfortune and the drone of the compound name of the deceased. He remembered it also because they sent them to play by the oak grove at O Polo, on the other side of the road, talking up the virtues of pelota, a game usually forbidden to them. He remembered that, on a day like this, somebody had died in Havana from a shot to the stomach and he had managed to suck secretly on the juice of the forbidden fruit.

That was when he had begun to walk with his eyes shut. At first it was only at night. He walked without switching on the lights, along the corridor that led to the bathroom. Using his fingertips, he made the journey, trying to accustom his eyes to the absence of light. On one of those nights he got a huge shock. He groped his way out of the door, as he usually did. He had barely reached the bathroom door when he felt a hand on his right shoulder. He started and began to yell like a man possessed. It was his father who had wanted to play a joke on him or teach him a lesson (he never found out which). The cries were followed by other cries, coming from all the other rooms. The house was a pandemonium of lights and of people running one way and another, faces distorted by the late-night vigil and longing to get to bed, the sooner the better. His father had turned into a hydra and been very strict in his punishment. For a start, no more getting up at night to go to the bathroom. He had to get used to going to the bathroom before bed, to form a habit and to pre-empt nocturnal emergencies. If he still had problems, the best thing was to keep a chamber pot under the bed and not go around scaring everybody like that. He had to have respect for others, blah-blah-blah. Furthermore, as a punishment, he would have to paint the garden fence. First clean it and paint it with red lead and then give it two coats of paint. They would talk about the colour tomorrow. Tomorrow he would have to start cleaning the railings. And now everybody had to go back to their rooms to try to piece together their sleep. They had had quite enough of shocks and interruptions.

Francis considered the punishment disproportionate, but had to resign himself to it. Insofar as the colour of the railings was concerned there was no mystery, he would paint them green, like they were now. In that house they were very traditional about colours and about everything. He dreamed all night of an immense set of railings that he was unable to finish painting. It was an immense night.

A few days later, subdued by the punishment, he changed tactic. Forbidden to go out at night, he decided to concentrate on his bedroom and as far as doing it at night – a decision that might just be a source of scandal – he decided that he could do the exercises by day. He tore a strip of black cloth from a sheet he found in a trunk and bandaged his eyes with it. He stayed like that for ever-longer periods, simulating a blindness that appeared again and again in his dreams. A total and absolute blindness that plunged him into a world of shadows. He walked from one side of the room to the other, avoiding the chairs and the corners of the bed, the curtains at the window and the armchair where he read the novels of Zane Grey, which he loved so much. He spent entire hours like that until one summer he decided the bandage made him very hot and decided to change his rituals.

He became obsessed then with using his left hand. He was right-handed through education and not by nature, because of his great-grandmother who said the left was the hand of the devil and that a child as good as Francisquiño must eat with his right, write with his right, cross himself with his right, do everything with his right like normal people who were all right-handed. Only evil people, witches and criminals were left-handed. God didn't want good children like Francisquiño to be left-handed. He tried then to go back to his natural side and began to use his left hand for almost everything. To shave and to open doors, to tie his shoelaces and to adjust his belt, to pick up the soap in the shower and to get money out of his wallet. Where he had never been left-handed was in masturbation, where he was right-handed. He carried on like that for a while until one day he tried to draw with his left hand and it came out as a scribble. There ended his potential career as a one-armed artist and there too began his cortical ambivalence, expanding the possibilities of his brain, with more contradictions than usual.

Now those behaviours seemed to him to be premonitions, indicators of a potential future marked by disabilities, signs of his possible future, unconscious and rather absurd omens of destiny. Now his eyes moistened while – beneath the vine, beside the washbasin, sitting in the wicker chair – he looked again and again, with the attention to detail of a style corrector, over the proofs of *Blindness*, the English version of *Ensaio sobre a Cegueira*, which he would shortly send to Martin, so he could relax, so Martin would stop pressuring him, and, most important of all, so he could fulfil the contract.

Rose tore into his daydreams, shouting that tea was ready, did he want some tea and biscuits?, and talking to him about how work was going, he had been sitting in that chair beneath the vine for ages, he had to get up and come to the kitchen, walk around a bit, stretch his legs.

The rest of the afternoon went past in a breath, absorbed as they all were in their tasks. When Luisa arrived with a fish pie to bake in the oven, the three of them looked at their watches to discover it really was almost nine at night.

The fish pie was splendid. Luisa had got the always tricky quantity of ginger just right, so that it was spiced without being spicy, so that their taste buds were submerged in the aroma without getting tired of it. Afterwards they moved on to an apple cake that Clodio had made with the Reinetas from the trees in the orchard, which rounded off a good-humoured meal watered with a delicious and refreshing wine from Ulla. They talked of almost everything that had happened in the world – a war, a kidnapping, floods in Europe and drought in Indonesia, another war and a catastrophe, thousands of people fleeing barbarism and rage – of the unbearable heat they were suffering that week, and how much that weather reminded them of Southern California.

They decided that the following day they would go to the beach, to swim and sunbathe, and picnic – potato tortilla and breaded steak, beer and ice cream – to take long walks, collecting shells and pebbles, and perhaps also to see the blue jellyfish drying out on the shore, to shake off the dust of routine and play at building castles on the sand.

The night was long and very hot. They opened the windows and made love with the lights off, as if they were blind.

When he finally made it to the beach Clodio was exhausted. He was holding Francis beneath the chin and swimming with one hand. Luckily he had brought the flippers, which helped him move in the water and gave his legs greater propulsion. When he touched sand, landing awkwardly on the beach like a marine mammal that had lost its way, he fell to his knees and called for help. Rose, who had been up to her knees in water for a while, scanning the horizon, her eyes wet with tears and fear, sped over to help Clodio. They were joined by three or four swimmers who had come over to see if they could help and to see what was happening, in solidarity, certainly, but also with a morbid anxiety, to see who the drowned man was, to see his distorted face, to feel themselves alive, observing the presence of death.

When they had got him out of the water – an inanimate bundle – there was, objectively, nothing to be done. His face was bloated, purple, cyanotic, and his heart, unquestionably, had ceased to beat. Nonetheless, in these cases nobody resigns themselves easily to not doing everything in their hands to find a solution, whether through prayer, as some of the older bystanders were doing, or by recourse to first aid and life-saving manuals, the sort we sometimes flick through in the doctor's waiting room or at school, at the Red-Cross centre or during the health-and-safety committee at our workplace. Then, the manuals need updating, or are not very clear, and the patron saints, not to say the divine beings, are occupied with other things and don't have enough guardian angels for so many people, because the demographic explosion in this world has caught those in the other world somewhat off guard, with all their chastity and all their angelic sex, and so there aren't enough of them for this great mass of whiners who want infinite protection, insurance against all risks and plenty of perks.

Clodio had read a life-saving manual, out of curiosity or precaution, before his first voyage and now he was trying every way he could to recall the images that (un)memory was revealing to him with what he perceived as exasperating slowness. He then tried mouth-to-mouth resuscitation and CPR, following a rhythm that was more invented than textbook. Meanwhile, Luisa, distressed by the situation, ran off, bellowing like a madwoman that she was going to find help, to call the emergency services and the police, the Red Cross or the fire brigade.

Clodio stretched out Francis's neck, put a hand on his forehead and joined his own mouth to that of the drowned man after clearing it out with his fingers. He breathed into him at a rhythm of a dozen times a minute, with one breath to every five pushes on the chest wall, level with the heart. He carried on like this for several minutes, not changing the rhythm or stopping even for a moment. The attempts, which anybody who wasn't desperately blind to what was happening could see would fail, were, after all, in vain.

When Luisa reappeared, pushing a path through the crowd that was milling around the scene, Clodio's face said it all. He hadn't done, could not do, anything. Francis was dead. Irredeemably dead. Drowned, staring, as if trying to steal the light illuminating the pupils of his eyes.

That was when Rose – who had been at Clodio's side throughout, not even blinking, helping with every push, breathing at every breath, putting on an obliging face – realized the epic magnitude of the tragedy, the finality of death, how lonely she was going to be without Francis, how lonely she was now, how heavy her legs were, how cold her lips and back, how terrible all of this was, how people were staring at her and the sobs, Clodio's face frozen on the point of dissolving, Luisa's attack of hysteria, Francis's violet and indigo and almost greenish face, how tight her bathing suit was, how unserious it was to be a widow in a yellow two-piece, how the ocean had changed colour from blue to grey, how much she loved Francis, and how Francis's eyes, open to infinity, lost in a different geometry, seemed greener and more alive than ever.

When you have seen a drowned man just pulled from the water, still laid out on the sand or at the side of the road, there isn't much you can say. It is always the same. You can't quite understand why people drown on particular days, when the waves aren't very strong and the sea is calm. Sometimes there are unforeseen situations, pins and needles in one leg or both (more serious), a stomach cramp, angina or something less organic but equally dangerous like a marine current, an attack from a dangerous animal, or being unable to resurface after getting caught in seaweed, down there where it forms forests or meadows. Other times the reason is unclear, when the drowned man himself wants to drown, when he enters the water, knowing he will not come out, does not want to come out, that he will remain beneath the water, ecstatic, blind, deaf, his open mouth gulping down the ocean, submerged, immersed, not breathing, dead. As for the rest, it doesn't matter if it is a man or a women, a child or an old person, it is always the same, the terrible stage-setting of classical tragedy. There are people around who put their hands to their head, others who begin to feel a cold sweat, and there is always somebody who is interested in the seaweed hanging around the drowned man's neck like a necklace of exquisite coral, or by the red stains around the wrists – lots of detective novels in summer, lots of thriller films in winter – or if he has a beard or is wearing an old-fashioned bathing suit.

When you have seen many drowned men, like the rescue services who arrive now to ascertain that they are too late, that they can do nothing, that the victim is anchored in that body lying on the sand, that this poor man is no longer a body but a cadaver, you always react the same way, with a mixture of disgust for the amphibian and distress at what has happened, at almost always arriving when there is nothing more to be done, when life is gone. The men of the emergency services knew immediately that those women were crying for something final, that the kneeling man, exhausted, with a glazed expression, had tried desperately to perform an impossible miracle, that the crazed girl had had an attack of hysteria and was, in fact, the most urgent case, that the rest of the people were in the way, unnecessary, annoying, that this was another number, an uncomfortable death that unbalanced the statistics.

When two men who were following the paramedics at a distance appeared with some stretchers and an air of calm, Clodio lowered all his defences and let himself be carried away by feeling, letting out a great wail of tears and sobs that he could not or would not halt. The bystanders began to make movements to regroup and withdraw. They left in groups of two or three, talking about the circumstances of the accident and bewailing the unfortunate man's fate. Others, still, were filling the air with calls to invented divinities or resorting to an eccentric roster of saints, imagined or real, some familiar, with their own saint's day, others of more obscure genealogy. Others even came over to Clodio and Rose, who, afflicted by the tragedy, had joined in a spastic embrace, as if they were afraid to part, as if they found refuge in one another's arms, as if they knew that the tragedy was beyond that embrace, and that when they parted reality would await.

Luisa was almost recovered, after the consolation of the bystanders and a tranquillizer pill the emergency services had given her, which hadn't had time to take effect but which suited Luisa fine, and suddenly she was the strongest and the most ready to face the situation. The paramedics, defeated and cold, were taking Francis to the hospital, to carry out an autopsy and find out the cause of death. A macabre routine, the product of administrative aloofness, of the law interpreted to its strictest point, when there is no doubt and only tears.

There was nothing left to do on that beach. The wind had swept round from the south-east, which in those latitudes was the sign of bad weather and a storm unleashed, and the waves were beginning to rise up with more force, as if wanting to emphasize their power, like an untamed meteor, the power of a nature that was not to be toyed with, of a furious, wild animal.

There was no time for grieving. From the hospital the body was taken straight to Santa María church. The funeral, with the body present, was very simple and, as one says in these cases, "there weren't many there." Because of his prolonged absence, Francis had maintained few friendships in his homeland and, although nearly all the people Francis would have wanted were there, it was a very small group. Clodio and Luisa, who could be considered family, Rose, of course, as companion and lover until the last frame, Martin, his publisher from San Francisco, he of the emergencies, the constant demands, the cold mind, who had asked as soon as he arrived – insensitive beast brought up in the basest ideology – for the tapescript or computer disk with the translation, a pair of childhood friends who had read about it in the newspaper, and Andy, who almost hadn't made it thanks to a strike on Northwest Airlines, who didn't make it, in fact, to see the body, but appeared in time to kiss a handful of earth and say the final farewell to his soulmate, his friend forever after.

When the ceremony ended, the first thing Andy did, trying to resist the impossible, with tears pouring in a waterfall from the inner corners of his eyes, sliding down his cheeks, entering his lips and mixing with the sob that was already coming out, liberated from its chains, budding like a flower, was to go over to Rose and embrace her hard, as he stuttered a kind of condolence.

"I'm so sorry, Rose. This wasn't the ending any of us wanted."

Rose reacted well, seeming maternal and welcoming. Somebody had to be strong in that extreme situation or everything would tumble down like a house of cards. She caressed Andy like what he was: a lost boy, a wandering soul shipwrecked on a sea of tears and pain.

"I know you feel it in a very special way. I know."

"Maybe you don't know everything."

Andy wiped away his tears and moved his head back to look at Rose, straight on, calmly, the source of his tears unexpectedly dry, enervated, intense, anxious for a response.

"If you're talking about you and Francis, I know."

Andy was surprised, as if feeling the dagger of betrayal going into his chest, as if thinking, with or without reason, that Francis had betrayed him, that he had revealed his secret. It rose up inside him and, moving away from Rose, he said drily:

"There's more. There's more that you don't know and will never know."

Rose reacted very badly, with irony extracted from the worst labyrinths of her mind, attacking with a low blow, despicable, causing hurt without a reason to somebody who does not deserve it, who is only nervous, who has travelled thousands of kilometres, who has suffered with every delay, with every cancellation, with every stopover in the airports of the world and who has not been able to see his best friend, his lifelong love, *forever and ever*, who has felt betrayed, naked, lost like a lost boy.

"Of course there's more. I also know you weren't the only one."

Clodio and Luisa came over to greet Andy, whom they hadn't had an opportunity to greet in the hurriedness of his arrival *in extremis*. Andy recoiling. Freeing himself at last from Rose's embrace. Wiping away his tears. Looking at her in confusion. Recomposing his face in an imaginary mirror. Feeling wounded, insignificant and ridiculous in his confidences. Clodio and Andy melted into an interminable embrace, of men who have lost their shyness, of disconsolateness and solidarity, of wounded soldiers who have lost a battle.

Luisa and Rose walked to the churchyard, leaving behind a pair of men sunk in a shipwrecked embrace.

"Don't let her torment you. She's very nervous and doesn't know what she's saying," Clodio murmured into Andy's ear.

"She's forgiven," said Andy, adopting an understanding and friendly tone. "Sometimes we all say things we don't think, not what we want to say."

"I knew him better than anybody. Since I was a lad and we would go out on the town together. He didn't love anybody more than he loved you. You can be sure. Completely sure."

Andy was moved and went back to wailing, which deconstructed him, turned him into human offal, a diminishing man, a caricature of himself. He sobbed and recomposed his face to speak to Clodio although he couldn't stop his bottom lip quivering, or tears assaulting him despite turning to look at the cypresses.

"Thanks, Clodio. I'd like to have heard it from his lips, but I heard it from yours and that means a lot."

Martin had booked into a hotel in Santiago to visit the city and its delights. The others went back to the family house. Nobody wanted to eat. Nobody wanted to talk or comfort anybody else. It was a night of monologues and solitary bodies, of darkness illuminated by the glimmer of eyes, of windows open in search of air, in search of shooting stars to make a wish on, and another, and another. For Francis. For everything to go well for him. For us to see one another again. For him not to have suffered. For it to be true that he loved me more than anybody else. For him to visit me in my dreams. It was the night that Rose and Andy slept in Francis's house for the last time.

It was difficult to wake up the next morning, after a night of insomnia and weeping. Rose and Andy came into the kitchen at almost the same time. They gazed at each other, eyes reddened from lack of sleep. They didn't speak. They only gazed at each other and forgave each other completely. They did it for Francis, to join together in his memory, so as not to violate his memory or seek out rivalries where they should never exist. Clodio and Luisa, who had slept apart, came in to complete the quartet, to speak little and look around softly at one another, united in pain and loss.

While the others were filing in and out of the bathroom, Rose looked out the disk with the definitive version of *Ensaio sobre a Cegueira*, *Blindness* in its English translation. In his diary Francis, always so organized with his notes, had left a comment: "Send the disk to Martin, for the initial proofs." She made the decision there and then to do this for him, since he could no longer do it for himself.

The farewell was simple. An embrace and a "see you soon" in which Rose and Andy tried to compensate for the pain they had caused each other. Andy's plane was leaving in the morning. Rose would leave in the evening, after putting things in order and picking out some souvenirs of Francis to keep for herself.

Clodio and Luisa took Andy to the airport. The farewell was restrained, quick, less traumatic than expected. In conversation they tried to be friendly and mundane, less sad and more positive. They invited Andy to come and stay with them whenever he liked. He did the same. They all knew they would never go, that this was a final farewell, that nothing remained to unite them, only the memory of Francis and an immense feeling of loneliness and loss, of abandonment and sadness.

On the plane, Andy opened an envelope that Clodio had given him moments before he passed through security. "From Francis," he had said falteringly, trying to stress the intimacy, the confidentiality, the affection and tenderness that those words carried. Inside was a single page, carefully folded in four. Opening it, Andy discovered a short poem by Francis. At the top it had a dedication, written in the tortuous and almost undecipherable handwriting that Andy knew so well, and which moved him almost as much as the typewritten text that followed: "For Andy, who doesn't know that I write him poems." It was a short poem, which Andy began to read in a murmur, until he reached the last verse, which he read out loud to the surprise of his neighbour:

> *Maidens and dragons*
> *Helmets, knights and swords*
> *Poppies, sunflowers*
> *In our living garden*
> *That suddenly sinks.*

He leaned against the window as the plane rose through a mass of clouds. Soon he would no longer see the countryside. Only clouds and then sea.

* * *

When a person goes blind, the world changes. Sometimes the mutation is so great that he recognizes absolutely nothing, not even the glass in the murderer's spectacles or the ideology he sustains. These are the problems of going blind, of losing focus, of thinking that one's inner world is the only world. Some blindnesses are contagious, they spread like epidemics to the four corners of the earth. Saramago wrote of it in a magnificent book, *Ensaio sobre a Cegueira*, which somebody once tried to translate and died, blind.

Read more fiction in English from Small Stations Press:

Xabier P. DoCampo, WHEN THERE'S A KNOCK ON THE DOOR AT NIGHT

The four stories in *When There's a Knock on the Door at Night* are made from materials that have entered into the author's ear and which he has made his own. On the surface, they may appear to be frightening, but they are only frightening until we open ourselves to them. They showcase the best of Galician storytelling in which events are told first-hand or related by someone who knows them and elements of the everyday intersect, criss-cross, with elements of the supernatural. Often the scene is a storm in the dark during which the traveller is forced to seek shelter for the night in a house where the story is told to him or he experiences the events himself. In "The Traveller's Mirror," a man on his way to reclaim his parents' estate is caught in a storm and attracted by the light of a forge, which he deduces is not a ghost because it remains still. On entering the blacksmith's house, he is struck by the similarity in their appearance – their faces are identical except for one detail. In "The Oven Man," an old woman in the village constantly plays tricks on or spreads rumours about her neighbours, reprehensible behaviour that leads three men to set out one night to teach her a lesson that goes badly wrong. In "The She-Wolf," a dandy who has never done a proper day's work in his life and who devotes himself to hunting and the pursuit of pleasure fails to fulfil a promise he has made, thereby provoking the injured party's fury and bringing down unfortunate consequences for all concerned. And in "Happy Death Day," a man receives cards, letters and other gifts in celebration not of the day he was born, but of the day he will die. He does everything in his power to escape this destiny before seemingly accepting his fate and succumbing to the inevitable. *When There's a Knock on the Door at Night* is a modern classic of Galician literature and received the Spanish National Book Award in 1995.

ISBN 978-954-384-087-8

Agustín Fernández Paz, NOTHING REALLY MATTERS IN LIFE MORE THAN LOVE

The ten stories in this magnificent collection "all talk of the importance of love, that feeling that can transform us more deeply than any other, and also of its absence, the void it leaves in people when the twists and turns of life make it impossible." So the author, Agustín Fernández Paz, writes in his afterword. A banker who, bored of the company of other directors, frequents a bookshop and is introduced to works she has never read before; a young man who falls in love with the daughter of the owner of the garage where he works; a man and a dog who continue to seek out the company of the Woman he loved; a couple who endure a freak accident, but only one survives; a woman who recalls her first, anxious physical contact with her boyfriend; a man who is proud of his collection of matchboxes; another who finds passport photos of the woman of his dreams on the pavement; the country house and its long-kept secrets; a woman whose life could have been so different had she followed the inclinations of her heart; and the man who comes up with the ingenious idea of advertising not services, but the openings of books that have transformed his life. There is in this work an analysis of the power of love over our lives, love that is requited and love that is left behind. There is also, as the author points out, a celebration of the positive impact that reading can have in our lives, and Fernández Paz very deliberately sets out to provide pointers to some of his favourite creators: Auster, Kafka, Pamuk and Rivas, Éluard, Neruda, Valcárcel and Valente, Hicks, Kar-

wai and Wenders... Readers will be able not only to sink into the charming prose of one of Galicia's most famous writers, but also to equip themselves with a to-do list of other authors. *Nothing Really Matters in Life More Than Love* received the 2008 Spanish National Book Award and is beautifully illustrated in colour by Pablo Auladell.

ISBN 978-954-384-086-1

Teresa Moure, BLACK NIGHTSHADE

Einés Andrade is a doctoral student whose studies center on the figure of the French philosopher René Descartes. But when she is only seven or eight, she is sent to the attic for calling her great-grandmother a monkey, and there she discovers a hutch, a large chest, from which emanate the scents of various herbs and fruits. She also discovers private papers belonging to Queen Christina of Sweden and a certain Hélène Jans, a herbalist and healer of Amsterdam. Digging deeper, she discovers that the two women shared a common passion. In 1649, Christina of Sweden invited Descartes to her court to give her lessons in philosophy, but he was reputed to have caught pneumonia and died in February, 1650. Before that, he had an affair—only once, as he claimed—with the maid of the bookseller in whose house he was staying in Amsterdam, Hélène Jans. She became pregnant and gave birth to their daughter, Francine, who died at the age of five in 1640. Fifteen years later, Queen Christina and Hélène meet to exchange impressions and ease their nostalgia. They strike up a correspondence in which Christina urges Hélène to continue her work on an artificial language, a language that can be easily learned and will serve to promote communication among different nations and prevent war. Hélène also puts together a recipe book, called *Book of Women*, in which she gives various remedies that can be used to alleviate pain in childbirth, to improve one's appearance, to attract a lover... Before she dies, she hands down her knowledge, the recipe book and her private papers, to her adopted daughter, Agnes, a distant ancestor of Einés's. Einés decides to abandon all research on rationalism and to devote her time to writing an account of these women whom Time has forgotten. *Black Nightshade*, which could just as easily have been titled *Chest in the Attic*, *Patchwork Quilt* or *Scent of Raspberries*, is an emblematic work by a leading writer of her generation, Teresa Moure, and was awarded the Xerais Prize for Novels in 2005.

ISBN 978-954-384-085-4

Anxos Sumai, THAT'S HOW WHALES ARE BORN

A young woman, who has left Galicia to go and study marine biology in Mexico (Baja California), is recalled to Galicia when it is found out that her mother is very sick. Her aunt would like her to sign some papers agreeing to take over the family business and renouncing her Mexican studies and emotional ties that she has forged in her new life. However, returning to Galicia and renewing her family ties is not exactly what the woman wants. Her mother has shut herself in her room for the last year, and relations between them have always been strained. She received more affection from a nanny, Felisa, and better advice from her uncle, Cándido. There is also an older brother, Ramón, a larger-than-life figure who has left an indelible mark in the lives of those around him, and an absent father. Will the woman's visit to see her sick mother turn out to be permanent, and will it soothe any of the festering wounds in her psyche, wounds that she has buried beneath her marine studies and a relationship with her one-time tutor? *That's How Whales Are Born* is a return to our origins, a search into the usefulness of stirring up past memories and seeking reconciliation.

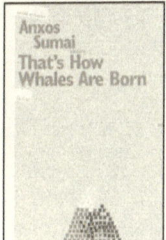

ISBN 978-954-384-073-1